6—
8/22

Interviewing Matisse

or

The Woman Who Died Standing Up

Interviewing Matisse

or

The Woman Who Died Standing Up

A NOVEL BY

Lily Tuck

ALFRED A. KNOPF   NEW YORK 1991

THIS IS A BORZOI BOOK
PUBLISHED BY ALFRED A. KNOPF, INC.

COPYRIGHT © 1991 BY LILY TUCK

LIBRARY OF CONGRESS CATALOGING-IN-
PUBLICATION DATA

TUCK, LILY, [DATE]
    INTERVIEWING MATISSE OR THE
    WOMAN WHO DIED STANDING UP : A
    NOVEL / BY LILY TUCK. — 1ST ED.
        P. CM.
    ISBN 0-394-58935-1
        I. TITLE. II. TITLE: INTERVIEWING
    MATISSE. III. TITLE: WOMAN WHO DIED
    STANDING UP.
    PS3570.U23615 1991
    813'.54—dc20   90-4917
                                            CIP

THIS IS A WORK OF FICTION. THE EVENTS
DESCRIBED HERE ARE IMAGINARY; THE SET-
TINGS AND CHARACTERS ARE FICTITIOUS
AND NOT INTENDED TO REPRESENT SPECI-
FIC PLACES OR LIVING PERSONS.

MANUFACTURED IN THE UNITED STATES OF
AMERICA

FIRST EDITION

TO EDWARD

I THANK GORDON LISH, MICHELLE HUNEVEN, SUZANNE MCNEAR, AND EDMÉE MONTANDON.

Probable nor'-east to sou'-west wind, varying to the southard and westard and eastard and points between; high and low barometer, sweeping round from place to place; probable areas of rain, snow, hail, and drought, succeeded or preceded by earthquakes with thunder and lightning.

—MARK TWAIN

Interviewing Matisse

or

The Woman Who Died Standing Up

Molly said, "She died standing up."

I said, "What?"

Molly said, "Standing up. Inez. Hello?"

I said, "Hello, Molly. Who? Inez?"

Molly said, "They found Inez propped up—propped up like a broom."

I said, "Inez? Like a what? A broom? God, Molly. What time is it?"

Molly said, "In the corner of the room. Inez was dressed in only her underwear. She was wearing boots."

I said, "Boots? Wait. Let me turn on the light, Molly. God, Molly, it's one o'clock in the morning. It's quarter past one in the morning, Molly."

Molly said, "Old fleece-lined boots. Do you know the kind I am talking about, Lily? The old-fashioned kind. Galoshes."

I said, "Galoshes? You woke me up, Molly. Hello?"

Molly said, "The kind of boots with buckles. The kind of boots you might wear in the snow or wear in the winter."

I said, "Winter? No, today is May twenty-third."

Molly said, "Yesterday. Yesterday was May twenty-third—Tuesday. Claude-Marie said they found Inez on Tuesday."

I said, "Where? Found Inez where, Molly? Oh, God, poor Inez."

Molly said, "Strange, isn't it? Isn't this the strangest thing you've ever heard, Lily? Not just about the boots, strange about

3

gravity. Gravity—I am not even going to get into gravity. And I am no scientist, Lily. But you don't have to be a scientist to know about gravity. Everyone knows about gravity. Little kids know about gravity. Still—I have never, no, I have never heard of anything like this—have you, Lily? Like Inez? Like someone dying standing up? Have you ever in your whole life? Lily? Hello? Are you there?"

I said, "Oh, God, Molly, are you calling me all the way from Connecticut?"

Molly said, "In her bra and her panties and Inez was wearing those boots, those galoshes, and Inez was standing right there as you stepped out of the old elevator. The decrepit old freight elevator—remember? Hello, Lily?"

I said, "Hello, yes. I am here. I am right here, Molly. You know what I thought of when the phone rang? I thought: Oh, my God, this may be Leonard."

Molly said, "I am not even in bed yet. I am not even undressed yet. What time did you say it was? Quarter past one?"

I said, "My watch is ten minutes fast. It's twenty after."

Molly said, "But what was I saying? Oh—the elevator— remember? You have to man that elevator yourself and no one is ever there to fix it if it stops or if it gets stuck. It did once. Yes, swear to God. The woman still in the elevator kept shouting: Get me out of here! I can hear her. I can hear her shouting clear as day and as if it were yesterday."

I said, "Oh, my God, Molly, Inez."

Molly said, "No, not Inez. The woman. The woman in the elevator, but yes, Lily—poor Inez. Yes. Inez was standing right there as you got out of the elevator and one of her arms was reaching out."

I said, "What? Inez's arm? Hello, Molly, I can hardly hear you. Can you speak into the receiver?"

4

Molly said, "Hello—is this better? Inez's arm was what I said and as if Inez was about to shake someone's hand or as if Inez had just finished shaking someone's hand only—and this was what Claude-Marie said. Claude-Marie said, you could have missed her—missed Inez. Claude-Marie said, if, for instance, you had stepped out of the old elevator really quickly because the old elevator had made it and you were relieved and you weren't really thinking and you walked into the room without really looking, the way people do, you could have walked right past her—past Inez was what Claude-Marie said."

I said, "Molly, Molly, I can still barely hear you. There is something wrong with this phone. I could barely hear Leonard either when he telephoned."

Molly said, "Lily, can you hear me now? I am shouting and my throat is going to get sore, and what I am talking about is how Claude-Marie said you could have walked right past her—past Inez—and how you could have walked right past the gardenia plants."

I said, "Gardenia plants? Oh, now I can hear you. I can hear you fine, Molly. It's the rain, maybe. It rained all day yesterday."

Molly said, "At least half a dozen gardenia plants—remember how all of them were always in bloom? Inez had a way with them—a green thumb was what. And remember, Lily, how Inez would sometimes put a gardenia in her hair? God, Inez had thick hair. God, how I envied Inez's hair. Lily?"

I said, "No, I love your hair. You have wonderful hair, Molly."

Molly said, "I am still sitting here at my desk and I cannot stop thinking—thinking about the gardenias and all the trouble Inez went to. The stand she had built for them especially. The stand right underneath the skylight and right where the plants

5

got all the light. Light is the one thing I do know, Lily. Light is important."

I said, "Poor Inez. I was sound asleep when you called, Molly."

Molly said, "Yes, poor Inez, but what I started to tell you was how Claude-Marie said you could have walked right past the gardenia plants and right past the big butcher block counter where Inez used to chop up the vegetables, and remember how Inez was also always talking to someone on the telephone? Inez had this extra long extension cord, and Inez could talk for hours on the phone—and as Claude-Marie said, you could have kept right on walking, walking past the couch, the second-hand couch Inez was always talking about and saying how she would get rid of it—throw the couch out—how she would put the couch out on the street for the bums to sleep on, and how she would buy another, a brand new leather couch that she had seen a picture of and that she had her heart set on."

I said, "The couch? Molly, this is what I said. I liked the couch. I kept telling Inez not to sell the couch. I kept telling Inez the couch was an antique—unique."

Molly said, "Claude-Marie said the stereo was on. The brand-new stereo was tuned to the station Inez always listened to. The one with practically no commercials, the one with almost continual classical music."

I said, "Oh, the stereo belonged to Kevin. I know the stereo belonged to Kevin, Molly. The speakers, though—the speakers belonged to Inez."

Molly said, "The bedroom was where Claude-Marie said you would have gone to next, Lily. You would have walked on past the couch to where the bathroom was and to where the bedrooms were. The bedroom Inez slept in and the bedroom she had let to Kevin, and Claude-Marie said you would have looked for Inez in there—in the bedroom—and you would have called out: Inez, Inez, where are you? Inez?"

I said, "Poor Inez."

Molly said, "This was what Claude-Marie said: Poor Inez dressed in only her underwear and wearing those old galoshes. You know what I said, Lily? I said to Claude-Marie: Don't forget the blue-and-white silk kimono Inez always wore. The kimono Malcolm brought back to Inez from the trip he took to Japan—to where was it, Lily—to Kyoto?"

I said, "Molly, I know, I know. I wore the kimono. I wore the kimono to a costume party. Molly, hello? I spilled *sake* on it."

Molly said, "I know what you are thinking, Lily. You are thinking what difference does the kimono make now, and it is too late anyhow—only this is how I always pictured Inez. Inez wearing a gardenia in her hair and Inez dressed in the blue-and-white silk kimono. And can't you see how Inez was always tucking in those sleeves and how those sleeves were always flapping and getting into Inez's way as she was chopping up the vegetables and as she was talking on the phone? I told Inez—I warned Inez over and over again—those sleeves could be a real liability for her."

I said, "But, Molly, you still haven't said who found Inez. Did what's-his-name Kevin find Inez?"

Molly said, "The delivery boy. A young boy delivering something. Dry-cleaning. The door was wide open, he said."

I said, "Oh."

Molly said, "The delivery boy called the police. Nothing, the police said, was missing. As far as they could tell, the police said, everything was in place. Claude-Marie said the same thing. Claude-Marie said thank God. And Claude-Marie said the first thing he thought of was the drawing hanging in the front hall—the drawing of Christ being taken down from the cross that Inez said she found in a second-hand store in Toledo and that she said was a Rembrandt, but that the expert from Sotheby's—or was he from Christie's? I don't remember—told Inez the drawing could be from the school of Rembrandt, but he didn't think so."

I said, "Molly, believe me, if that drawing is a Rembrandt, I'll eat it."

Molly said, "What? Oh, the Inca hats Price brought back from Peru, too. The hats Price said were valuable and Inez said were just dustcatchers. And the silverware. Nothing was missing. Oh, and all those appliances, remember? The appliances lined up right there on the butcher block counter where you couldn't miss them—the Cuisinart, the espresso machine, the machine to make pasta. Oh, and remember how Inez used to complain that all the instructions were written in a foreign language and she could not understand them? The brand new stereo was right there, too. No one had touched the stereo. I told you, the stereo was still on, the stereo was playing."

I said, "Molly, I am sure the stereo belonged to Kevin."

Molly said, "Oh, WQXR. Lily, WQXR is the station Inez always listened to. Oh, and have I mentioned this? Have I told you this already, Lily? What Price told Claude-Marie the coroner said when he examined Inez? The coroner said he found drugs in Inez's blood."

I said, "Drugs? Is that what you said, Molly? Oh, my God, Inez didn't—hello? Molly?"

Molly said, "No, no, Lily. I—Price did not think so either. Price mentioned this right away. This and the boots. Price said the boots were definitely not *his* boots. Claude-Marie said Price said that black cowboy boots would have been different.

Price told Claude-Marie that he had had the black cowboy boots ever since he was a boy and sixteen years old and the boots still fit him. The boots, Price said, had a lot of meaning for him, and Claude-Marie said when he heard this, that he told Price that he knew just what Price meant. He, Claude-Marie, said he was French, and that he used to have a pair of shoes that he had bought at a store right off the Place de la Concorde right after the war, and, to him, Claude-Marie, the shoes were a kind of a symbol for him. A symbol, Claude-Marie said, that the war was over, although the shoes were actually made in Italy."

I said, "Oh—Italian shoes. Italian shoes fit me the best."

Molly said, "Only what I said to Claude-Marie was this, Lily. I said: Inez never took drugs in her life. No. Inez did not drink either. Sometimes, Inez drank a little wine—a glass of white wine. I told Claude-Marie: Inez would not even swallow an aspirin. The time Inez got the flu—the flu with the funny name that everyone got one winter. Claude-Marie got it, too. Claude-Marie got a high fever, and Claude-Marie said he ached all over, and Claude-Marie said he felt as if a bunch of wild horses had kicked him, and I was lucky. I was lucky I didn't catch the flu from Claude-Marie that winter."

I said, "Oh, you mean the Asian flu? Is that what you mean, Molly? Leonard got really sick from it—a high fever, aching, aching all over, those were his symptoms."

Molly said, "Inez took only this homeopathic medicine—little white pills you let melt on your tongue that have no taste—that taste the same—and Kevin kept telling Inez it was all psychological."

I said, "Who? Kevin? Please, Molly, don't talk to me any more about Kevin."

Molly said, "Lily, Kevin was all Inez ever talked about.

9

Kevin this and Kevin that and how much, she, Inez liked him, how much she, Inez, loved him, how she, Inez, was in love with Kevin. I could never even get a word in edgewise, and Inez said how it was all right there in her astrological chart. And astrology, remember, was something else Inez always talked about. Inez said how by just looking at the position of the stars and the planets, she could tell. Inez could tell, she said, what would happen, and ninety-nine per cent of the time out of a hundred Inez said these things happened and she was right. All the stuff about the divorce and Price and about Kevin—Inez said she could have predicted this and that it was all right there in her chart."

I said, "Molly, I am a Libra, and Inez was—what was Inez? Inez was born in June. Price, remember, Molly, gave Inez the surprise birthday party."

Molly said, "Oh, yes, the party, and Price was the one who telephoned Claude-Marie last night. And Price, according to what Claude-Marie told me, would not go and identify Inez at the morgue. If he did, Lily—that was what Price said to Claude-Marie—this would be the way, he, Price, would re-member Inez for the rest of his life. Price told Claude-Marie he did not want this. Price told Claude-Marie he wanted to remember Inez another way—alive, I guess. And Price's new wife didn't want Price to go either, and Price asked Claude-Marie. Claude-Marie had to go to the morgue. Claude-Marie had to drive to the morgue all the way from Connecticut, and too bad, too, it is raining, was what I said to him."

I said, "You're right. You should see it now. It is pouring, Molly."

Molly said, "Because of the rain, Claude-Marie is not going to drive home again, Lily. Claude-Marie telephoned. Claude-Marie telephoned right after he had been to the morgue, and

Claude-Marie said how Inez must have been there a while, and how they had to break her arm—Inez's outstretched arm, the arm I was telling you about. Rigor mortis, Claude-Marie said, had set in."

I said, "Rigor mortis?"

Molly said, "The boots, too. The galoshes. And you know what Price did? First thing, Claude-Marie said, Price did was to call the bar—the bar where Kevin worked part-time weekday nights. What's the name of the bar, Lily? The Something Something Avenue Bar?"

I said, "You mean the bar right across from—oh, and who was it who told me he went there once and who should be in there drinking a beer by herself but Faye Dunaway?"

Molly said, "Who? Was Faye Dunaway the one in that movie where Jack Nicholson gets his nose sliced open with a razor blade? Did you see it, Lily? Ugh, it was awful. In the end, Faye Dunaway is slumped over the steering wheel and the horn—but what was I saying? Oh, yes, Claude-Marie. Claude-Marie said Price talked to a waitress named Diane, and Price said he talked to someone else too, at the bar. Both Diane and the other person, Claude-Marie said, told Price the same thing. The bar, too, was so noisy and crowded, Price told Claude-Marie, that he, Price, could not hear a thing."

I said, "You mean *Chinatown*, Molly. I saw the movie with Jim in San Francisco, which was a coincidence."

Molly said, "And did I tell you what else Price said? Claude-Marie said Price said he could tell by just looking at Kevin what kind of bartender Kevin was. I know what Price means, Lily. I could tell, too, by how Kevin lounged around all day on the couch—the same couch Inez wanted to throw out—and how Kevin wore nothing but a pair of old running shorts and Kevin did not run. No. Price ran. Price ran a marathon once, remember? Kevin used to just sit there and ask Inez to bring him his stuff—his cigarettes, his beer, her ass once. Poor Inez. And Inez said she was allergic to smoke, to cigarette smoke, and I remember the time Inez's mother was smoking a—oh, have you met Inez's mother, Lily? You met her at the birthday party, and Inez's mother is not at all the way I pictured Inez's mother to be or the way Inez was. No, no. Inez's mother is blond, Inez's mother is remarried, Inez's mother chain smokes, and the time I am telling you about now, Lily, Inez kept getting up from where she was sitting and opening up the window, and this was in winter and this was after Price had left—after Price and Inez had separated already, but before Price had remarried yet—and Inez kept telling her mother how she was going to ruin and kill off the gardenia plants with her cigarette smoke and Inez's mother kept telling Inez how Inez was going to kill *her* off with pneumonia if she did not sit down right this minute and shut the window. Hello?"

I said, "Hello—yes. I am sure I met Inez's mother at the birthday party, Molly. Inez's mother lives in New Jersey, she said."

Molly said, "Yes, but one thing, though—the thing Inez and her mother had in common—they both liked to talk on the phone a lot. I'll never forget this, Lily, and this was what Inez told me and, swear to God, this is true and what Inez said to me. Inez said, that when she, Inez, was little, her father had tried to call, call home from his office, and the phone was busy all morning. So, Inez's father got into his car and he drove all the way back home—this was still in Wisconsin—and without a single word to Inez's mother, who was still talking on the phone, Inez's father yanked the phone, wire and all, right out of the wall. He left a big hole there, and he never once said a word to Inez's mother, and what Inez said was that as long as she lived, she, Inez, would never forget the hole in the wall where the phone was."

I said, "Molly, a lot of men are like this. Sam, Molly. Sam would do this. He would, Molly. Sam, I swear, would do something just like this, Molly."

Molly said, "Oh, and Inez's father was the one who died of a heart attack, Lily. Now, it's all coming back to me. Did you hear this already, Lily? Inez's father died of a heart attack in someone—no, not in Inez's mother's arms—in some other woman's arms, and Inez told me how even now she still could not stop thinking about this. Inez told me how she, Inez, was only twelve then, and how she was away on a school camping trip where the whole class had to hike up all the way to this lake, and Inez also said how she did not want to go on this trip and—no—not because Inez had any kind of presentiment—no—because she didn't like these school camping trips. Inez said she hated sleeping outdoors. She always caught poison ivy, she said, and Inez said, she had tried to talk her mother into letting her not go and stay home, and when she got back, back from the camping trip, Inez said, not only was her father dead, he was not there. He was gone."

I said, "But what about the other woman, Molly? Who was she, do you know?"

Molly said, "Lily, funny—I asked Inez the very same thing. I asked Inez if her father was really in love with this woman. And Inez said she did not know either, only she could not stop thinking about it. With Price, too, Inez said. When she and Price were making love was what Inez said she meant. Each time she and Price made love, Inez said, she could not stop thinking about what if Price had a heart attack right there on top of her, even if Price was only her husband."

I said, "Like Rockefeller. Remember what's-his-name Rockefeller, Molly? Nelson. Nelson Rockefeller."

Molly said, "Yes, Nelson, but what was I saying? What was I talking about, Lily?"

I said, "Inez. You were talking about Inez, Molly."

Molly said, "Oh, yes, Inez. I was talking about Inez, and I was saying how I should have warned Inez. I should have told her what Price said about Kevin. About how Kevin was the kind of bartender who uses shot glasses with phony measuring rings so that it looks to everyone like he is pouring out a lot more than he is and a lot more than just an ounce—oh, and did I tell you this, Lily? Kevin left a whole bunch of stuff—old paperbacks and magazines, a pair of jeans, some T-shirts, one good dress shirt with French cuffs. His toilet kit, too, Price said. Price told Claude-Marie he found the toilet kit in the bathroom. The toilet kit was filled with Kevin's toothbrush and stuff, an electric razor and a package of condoms, and Price's new wife, Claude-Marie said, threw everything out, and Price's new wife wore rubber gloves. Rubber gloves, swear to God, this is true, Lily. Claude-Marie said he was there, and Claude-Marie said Price and Price's new wife would not touch any of Kevin's stuff. The two kids would not either."

I said, "Who? Molly, who? You are fading again. Speak into the receiver, will you?"

Molly said, "Hello? Can you hear me, Lily? Inez's two kids. Inez's two boys. Price Junior had to fly in from San Francisco—San Francisco is where he lives now—the other boy is still in school. In Colorado, in Denver, I think. Or is it Boulder? Boulder, Colorado, Lily. And Claude-Marie said to me I would never have recognized these two boys. The two boys have grown so. Grown, I suppose, the way Bibi, my own daughter, has grown. This year, Bibi is going to be fourteen. I can't believe this either."

I said, "Fourteen? Molly, I can remember when Bibi first started school and she had to wear the little blue uniform."

Molly said, "Poor Bibi. Bibi hates living in Senlis with Dominique, Claude-Marie's sister, and Lily, just stop and think for a minute—think of how long it has been. It has been over ten years now since we moved into the house on rue Madame."

I said, "Molly, hard to believe, isn't it? And I was still married to Jim. We were living in the apartment with no hot water overlooking the Parc Monceau."

Molly said, "The same year Price came to Paris to look at the site for his sculpture. No, it must have been the year after, Lily—the year I had all my hair cut, and Price—I'll never forget this either, Lily—Price always wore this wool jacket, this red-and-black-plaid jacket like the jackets lumberjacks wear, and Price wore the jacket all over Paris. Price never took off the jacket—not even inside a restaurant."

I said, "I haven't seen Price in months. I haven't seen Price since Yuri's opening and we went to the Vietnamese restaurant."

Molly said, "Claude-Marie sees Price. Claude-Marie sees Price all the time at the gallery and you know how tall Price is, Lily? Much taller than Claude-Marie. Price is head and shoulders taller than Claude-Marie, and Price, I remember, towered over everyone else along the Boulevard Montparnasse, and I remember I was telling Price how Gide, Malraux and Sartre had sat in those cafés—the cafés on the Boulevard Montparnasse—the Coupole and the Rotonde and the other one, the Dôme, and when Price and I got as far as the Closerie des Lilas, I told Price how the Closerie des Lilas was Hemingway's favorite restaurant and how Hemingway always used to eat there, and Claude-Marie, I think, must have been away for the weekend then—Claude-Marie must have been in Senlis visiting Dominique, his sister—and Price and I had a drink there—a drink at the Closerie des Lilas—and at the time, I had no idea who Inez was or that Price was married. Hello?"

I said, "Hello, yes. I can hear you. Molly, you know what time it is? It is nearly a quarter to two in the morning."

Molly said, "Yes, and Inez said she and Price got married too young. Inez said she and Price got married straight out of high school. One week after their high school graduation. And Inez told me how she had given up everything so Price could paint, so Price could sculpt. But what Inez said she really blamed Price for was for sneaking around her back with what's-her-name—with Price's new wife. Oh, why can't I remember the woman's name, Lily? Price's new wife's name is on the tip of my tongue—a funny name. A nickname. Nora would know. I can ask Nora. She and Nora take the same yoga class. Price's new wife is a whole lot younger was what Nora also said. And from the very beginning, Claude-Marie said, he did not want to take sides. Claude-Marie said he did not want to be in the middle. What could I do, Lily? What could I say to Inez? In the restaurant. The last time I saw Inez, Lily. When was this? Two weeks ago when Inez and I had lunch together and it was raining."

I said, "Where, Molly? Which restaurant are you talking about?"

Molly said, "The Italian restaurant. The Italian restaurant I went to with Yuri once—the time Yuri came to New York for his opening. The time Nora complained about. Inez and I, I remember, we were the very last ones to leave the restaurant. The waiters were scraping the chairs and setting up the tables, and the whole time too, Inez just kept talking—talking and telling me how she loved Kevin and how after Kevin left in the evenings, she could not get to sleep and how she could not resist it. Inez could not help herself was what Inez said to me. Inez said she went down the street and around the corner to the bar and to where Kevin worked part-time at night, and Inez said she would watch Kevin from the window, in the dark and from outside in the street. Inez told me she watched how Kevin made the drinks and how he talked to the waitresses, and Inez said how she hated herself. Inez told me how she would wait for Kevin to come home at two or three o'clock in the morning and she made love to him whether, at first, Kevin wanted to or not. Inez told me how she, Inez, would do anything for Kevin. Inez said how she would crawl naked on her hands and knees to the door of his bedroom—the door of her bedroom, Lily—because, of course, after the first couple of days, Kevin no longer paid any rent."

I said, "What? No rent? Kevin did not pay any rent, Molly? How much rent was Inez asking, Molly?"

Molly said, "Lily, the rent made no sense. I said so myself. I said this to Inez. So did Patricia—Patricia, Inez's sister. Patricia told Inez that if Inez were she, Patricia, Kevin would have to pay every bit of the rent, every last penny of the rent. Patricia told Inez that Kevin would also have to share the utilities, the gas and the electricity, and when I told Claude-Marie this, Claude-Marie said he agreed. Claude-Marie said he agreed completely with what Patricia had said to Inez. Also, Claude-Marie has a thing about electricity. Because of the war, I guess, Lily, Claude-Marie is always turning off the lights—turning them off after me and after everyone, even if, say, I am just leaving the room for a minute to go to the bathroom, even if I am planning to return to the room almost immediately. I don't know how many times I have told Claude-Marie not to and besides, it is not always so economical the way Claude-Marie says it is. Like stopping and starting a car to save gas, which everyone knows is a fallacy."

I said, "I know what you mean, Molly. I told you about when Jim and I were crossing the desert and I said to Jim: Jim, for once in your life, please listen to me."

Molly said, "Which reminds me of the other thing Claude-Marie said when he telephoned—no, not the first time—when Claude-Marie telephoned from Ivan and Nora's apartment—this is where Claude-Marie is right now, where Claude-Marie is spending the night—on Ivan and Nora's sofa bed. The same sofa bed Yuri slept on, and what I was going to say was how Claude-Marie and Price and damn—damn, why can't I remember the woman's name? It's driving me crazy, Lily."

I said, "Go through the alphabet. Start with A—Abigail, Alice, Ann; then B—Barbara, Bea—"

Molly said, "I'll think of her name in a minute—but what Claude-Marie said was Price still had a set of keys, and Price told Claude-Marie he did not want to go there alone. So Price, and Price's new wife whatever her name is, and Claude-Marie, all three of them went, and this was what I was going to tell you, Lily—what Claude-Marie said he had noticed from way down in the street. Claude-Marie said he noticed all the lights were on and not just the stereo, the way I said, Lily. The dry-cleaning too. The dry-cleaning, Claude-Marie said, was lying right there on the floor as you stepped out of the old elevator. The dry-cleaning was lying right under the picture of Christ being taken down from the cross and right where the delivery boy had dropped it probably, when he saw Inez. Poor Inez. No one, Claude-Marie said, had bothered to turn off the lights or turn off the stereo, and no one—not the police even—had bothered to pick up the dry-cleaning, which in a way, Claude-Marie said, was ironic. The dry-cleaning was someone else's tuxedo, Lily, and—oh, the delivery boy told the police, at first, he thought Inez was one of those statues—one of those life-sized statues like the one on Park Avenue, the one of a man hailing a taxi—Lily?"

I said, "Yes—by George Segal."

Molly said, "But I should have guessed, Lily. This is what I kept thinking. This is what I kept saying to myself—I should have guessed in the restaurant—I told you already, Inez kept me waiting and it was raining—oh, and you should have seen what Inez was wearing, Lily. Inez was wearing T-shirts—a whole bunch of T-shirts that were layered one on top of each other and all of them were different colors—oh, and this reminds me, Lily, Inez gave me a T-shirt to take back to Bibi. A T-shirt that says *Shit Happens* on it that Claude-Marie said Bibi could not wear and that I said: In France, it does not matter. In France, I said to Claude-Marie, no one knows what *shit* means, and Claude-Marie said: No, in France, people do know. But what was I saying? Oh, Inez was also wearing this scarf. A yellow gauzy silk scarf that Inez had tied turban style and that covered her hair—her thick hair. The scarf had these little gold bangles sewn on the ends gypsylike and the little gold bangles kept shaking and shining while Inez kept talking and telling me about Kevin and telling me how she wanted to travel, too, and how she had never been anywhere except for that one time to Spain with Price, and Spain, Inez said, had been a mistake, and I said: Inez, I only have the five hundred dollars to lend you."

I said, "Five hundred dollars? What five hundred dollars, Molly?"

Molly said, "I told you, didn't I, how I told Inez I couldn't lend her the money she asked me for and how I said: Please believe me, Inez, I don't have a thousand dollars. I said: Inez, don't forget, we have to sell the house in Connecticut. And I said: No, no, no—it's not all Claude-Marie's fault. Inez, I don't blame Claude-Marie. I blame Thomas Hamlin Aldrich."

I said, "Who, Molly? Thomas who?"

Molly said, "Claude-Marie's broker. But this is a whole other story. I am not even going to get into Thomas Hamlin Aldrich with you, Lily. Anyhow, it is too late now. Thomas Hamlin Aldrich was electrocuted to death when his dog peed against a lamppost. This is true—swear to God. The dog died too. The wires were not grounded or insulated or whatever they have to be. This was what I told Inez. I told Inez how Claude-Marie went to the funeral, and how Claude-Marie said the church was packed although most of the people there were just like him probably—like Claude-Marie—broke. And I told Inez how I had so much to do still. I said I have to sell this house in Connecticut, I said I have to pack up our stuff. I have to pack up the cat. You don't like cats, do you, Lily? And you should see my desk, Lily. The desk I am sitting at right this minute as I am talking to you. I have saved nearly everything—bills, letters, recipes, clippings, things out of newspapers—everything."

I said, "But Molly, what about Inez and the money?"

Molly said, "Five hundred dollars so-help-me-God-or-strike-me-dead was all I said to Inez I could lend her—oh, this was what the only other married man said to me too, Lily, only he said this to me about his wife. The only other married man besides the French count said he had not slept with— he had not had sex with his wife in nearly ten years and not since the time we landed the astronauts. He said he remembered this distinctly. He said he had watched this on TV and he remembered, he said, how they, the astronauts—had walked on the moon without gravity, how they had looked as if they were floating. He remembered too, he said, how hard it was for them to step up and back up into their capsule, and how after that he and his wife had made love, and that time, he said, was the last time they had done this—so-help-him-God-or-strike-him-dead."

I said, "I watched the same program, too, Molly, and to me, the moon landing did not seem real. To me, the moon landing looked made up in a studio and Sam—Sam, who was watching the program with me—said just like Orson Welles."

Molly said, "Who? But Inez—I'll never forget. Inez was in Spain then, and Inez said she only saw the picture later in *Life* magazine, and what else did she say? Inez said at the time—the same time—she did not know how a good Catholic girl like herself could go to bed with someone named Jesus, and I said to her: Inez, wait a minute. The Spanish, Inez, all have names like Jesus and Immaculate Maria. The Spanish, I said, all go to bed with each other. Oh, and Ramirez. Ramirez was what Inez said. Inez said she would always remember this—how everyone in the village outside of Toledo was named Ramirez and how they were all related and how everyone in the village always wore black and how no one said a single word to her for the entire year and all Inez did was lug the kids and the groceries up this steep hill to where they lived the year Price got the grant. But where was I? Oh—in the restaurant. But first, did I tell you, Lily? Did I tell you Inez arrived half an hour late? My shoes, too, my shoes were soaking wet, it was pouring, pouring just the way it is today. I was all set to go back—back to Connecticut—and when Inez finally arrived, guess what? Inez arrived in a taxi. If Inez needed the money, Inez could have taken the bus, Inez could have taken the subway. Instead—oh, Inez also had an argument with the taxi driver. An argument over the fare. Inez said *fuck you* to the driver and the driver laughed. He said *dosvidanya.*"

I said, "Oh, the driver must have been Russian, Molly."

Molly said, "But, Lily, I am trying to remember what else Inez said besides how she and Price got married straight out of high school, only a week after their high school graduation, and how she, Inez, gave up everything so Price could paint, so Price could sculpt, and how, in this village, all she did was wash—wash out clothes, wash out diapers—and there was no one in the village for her to talk to except for this one boy who babysat—Jesus Ramirez. And Jesus, Inez said, was really only a child. Jesus, Inez said, was maybe fourteen or fifteen years old, and the time Inez was talking about—the time the astronauts landed—Price was out. Price had gone to Toledo to buy paint brushes, to buy art supplies. Inez was at home alone, she said. Inez said she was washing out clothes and the water was running. Well, nearly alone. The two boys were there. But the two boys did not count. The two boys were little, Inez said. The two boys were napping, which makes me wonder out loud, Lily, what those two boys look like right now—right this minute, I mean. The older boy, Price Junior, I know, looks just like Price. The younger boy, the boy who was nearly born in the car, doesn't look like anyone. Matthew does not look like either Inez or Price—oh, yes, except once—once Inez said, if Matthew were to put on a bow tie, Matthew would look just like her father. Inez's father. The one who died of a heart attack. The one whom I was just telling you about. He, her father, Inez said, always wore a bow tie, a polka dot bow tie. Oh—this makes me wonder too, Lily, about the poor woman—remember? The poor woman whose arms he died in? I wonder about how she would have had to get Inez's father dressed again. How she would have had to put on Inez's father's socks and put on his vest—if, that is, Inez's father had worn a vest—and how she would have had to tie the bow tie and how she probably had never tied a bow tie in her life and how she probably had to tie the tie a dozen times before she thought she got it right and was halfway satisfied."

I said, "Molly, I know. Sam tried to teach me how to tie a bow tie. It's not easy, Molly. Sam made me practice on my knee."

Molly said, "Strange too, what this makes me think of. This makes me think of my own father. My own father did not wear bow ties, Lily, and my father did not die of a heart attack. My father died of an aneurism sitting right there at his desk, and what this makes me think of is how my father said he wanted to be cremated. Cremated in his white linen suit, he said. A suit he had had made to measure in England—especially. Only when he died, the suit no longer fit him. My mother had to have that white linen suit altered, Lily. I tried to talk my mother out of it—out of letting out the suit. I told my mother if my father was going to be buried this would have been different. My mother said I was hard-hearted and, what was more, I had no respect for the dead. I said to her: After all, I am just trying to be practical, and when I told Claude-Marie—told Claude-Marie what my mother had said—Claude-Marie said he knew all along anyway that all Southerners were crazy. Virginians. Virginians is what I keep reminding Claude-Marie, and I keep telling Claude-Marie there is a big difference. Virginians, I tell Claude-Marie, are not Southerners. Virginians are different. I had the same discussion with Yuri once. Yuri is Russian, and Russians, too, are different. In a way, Lily, Russians are a lot like Virginians. I told Yuri he, Yuri, would have loved my mother. Only you cannot believe everything Yuri says—for instance, about his own mother. Yuri is always saying how his mother knew Chekhov, and Chekhov, we all know, died in 1904, which would mean that Yuri's mother was over a hundred years old—oh, like Havier's grandmother. You know my friend Havier in Old Saybrook—Havier who helped me with the seagull, Havier who is Fred's lover? According to Havier, his grandmother has nineteen children, sixty-four grandchildren, and God knows how many great grandchildren, and Havier, because he is gay, is the only one in his family, he says, except for one sister, who has something wrong with her ovaries, not to have any children. Inez—when I told her this—Inez could not believe this. Inez only has the one sister—Patricia. And Patricia has no children. Patricia, Inez said, had electroshock treatment. Patricia moved to Hawaii. Lily? Electroshock treatment, Lily, is not as bad as it sounds and a lot of people I know have had it. Amy, my best friend from school in Charlottesville, has. Amy had electroshock treatment because she saw monkeys— monkeys instead of people. Oh, did I say Charlottesville, Lily? I said Charlottesville because Charlottesville is simpler. I lived in a small town outside of Charlottesville. But Crozet is not really a small town either. Crozet is a bunch of houses, a general store, a post office. What's more, no one has ever heard of Crozet, and if Claude-Marie thinks all Southerners are crazy, Claude-Marie should have lived in Crozet. Claude-Marie should have met the Miss Marys, which reminds me of the town Kevin said he was from—LeGrange, Texas."

I said, "Molly, it is two o'clock. Two o'clock in the morning. There is not much we can do now, is there?"

Molly said, "No, no, you are right, Lily, only I can't stop thinking. Thinking about Kevin, and how by then, Inez said, she was desperate. The ad too, Inez said, was expensive and when the phone rang, Inez said, she nearly did not answer it. Inez said she had given up hope. Inez said she was at the end of her rope. I know. I put an ad in the paper once—the *Old Saybrook Star*—an ad for kittens. For three days, the ad cost me sixty-five dollars, and Claude-Marie said I was crazy. The ad too, Claude-Marie said, was too wordy, and I told Claude-Marie I was just trying to be accurate and to find good homes for the kittens. You know how I feel about kittens, Lily? How I feel about animals? Europeans—Claude-Marie, for instance—do not have the same sensibility. Take Suzanne, for example. Before Suzanne and Harry moved away to Santa Fe, Suzanne always took in strays. Suzanne, remember, Lily, lived next door to us, then the Thomases bought her house. Now, someone else has moved in there whom I haven't met yet and who, Claude-Marie says, is the spitting image of Mercedes. Oh—you met Mercedes, didn't you, Lily? Mercedes is Nora's sister. Mercedes came to New York from Bogotá or Bolivia, and the funny thing, come to think of it, was Nora also tried to call Inez. Nora tried to call Inez to rent the room for her sister. For Mercedes. Actually, it was me. I tried to call Inez that day—oh, that awful day. The day I shall never forget, Lily. And, of course, I was not home either when Claude-Marie, Ivan, and Nora got there. Claude-Marie said how they had to take a taxi, a taxi from the train station in Old Saybrook, and Claude-Marie said he thought the trouble was the car. Claude-Marie thought the car would not start. Claude-Marie had bought a new battery, and Claude-Marie thought this was the reason why I did not come to the station to fetch them. But it wasn't the car, it was the cat. I told you how I stopped driving then. I refuse ever to drive again. And the reason is, Lily, each time I see a cat, the cat turns into a child. A child just like Bibi, even though Bibi is almost fourteen and Bibi is almost taller than I am now. Can you blame me? The other thing I keep thinking about is: Was it because I was in reverse? Have I told you this already, Lily? Have I told you how I was backing out of the driveway and how first I was on my way to the grocery store before picking up Claude-Marie—Claude-Marie, Nora and Ivan—at the station? The cat must have been lying under the car, and what still troubles me is my reaction. Instead of putting on the brakes, I pushed down harder on the accelerator. Oh, God, and what was it Ivan said? Ivan said this was a normal reaction while wouldn't-you-know-it Claude-Marie never stopped talking about the car. There was nothing the matter with the car. Oh, yes, maybe, the fender, a little. Oh, you have met Ivan, haven't you? Ivan and Nora. Ivan escaped from a gulag in Russia. I met Ivan at Yuri's opening. Afterwards, we all went to this Vietnamese restaurant Claude-Marie said was the 'in' restaurant to go to. Inez was there, too. Inez sat next to Yuri, and this was when Yuri told everyone about his mother, about how his mother had known Chekhov, and Inez, I remember, said how she loved Chekhov."

I said, "Molly, have you forgotten? I told you, I was there. I was at the Vietnamese restaurant. I sat next to Malcolm, and Price was sitting at the other end of the table with what's-her-name, his new wife, only they were not married yet."

Molly said, "Price. Yes, of course, Price. Price met Yuri the time Price came to Paris. As a matter of fact, Price and Yuri were both in the car with Claude-Marie, me, and Bibi —Bibi was in the car too, then—when the plane crashed. This was before I met Inez. I met Inez the same year my mother had to have surgery. The year I had to fly back from Paris on one day's notice, I'll never forget this, Inez—the first time I met her—was sunbathing on the roof. Inez was sunbathing nude. In July. I am certain about the month, Lily. The tar on the roof was melting in kind of silvery pools. I also remember how the World Trade Centers looked like two giant pieces of aluminum foil, and I remember how little rivulets of sweat were streaming down Inez's naked belly and the sweat was full of little black soot specks. Mostly, I remember how I have never been so hot in my life. I am not kidding, Lily. God, it was hot. Also, I was jet-lagged. Hello?"

I said, "Hello. Yes, I'm here. New York in July is terrible, Molly. July and August, Molly."

Molly said, "I flew over from Paris on one day's notice. My mother, Lily, was in the hospital—the Martha Jefferson Hospital—oh, and the turbulence. I will never forget the turbulence on that flight, Lily. The plane bucked its way across the Atlantic Ocean and not once during the entire flight, not once during the seven-and-a-half hours, did they ever turn off the seat belt sign. Not once. I swear, Lily. They could not serve lunch or dinner or whatever the meal was. Midway somewhere, midway across the ocean, I suppose, the pilot apologized. The pilot promised us, the passengers, a coupon. A coupon for a free meal at the airport, a free cocktail too, he said. The pilot announced this over the intercom, and I may still have the coupon here somewhere—somewhere here in my desk. I told you, Lily, I keep everything. I may have kept the note I wrote then as well. I remember, I put the note in my pocket, next to my wallet and next to my passport— you know me, Lily, I hate to fly. I am afraid of people screaming and clutching at things, I am afraid of disorder and mayhem, afraid of disfigurement and dismemberment, and if I could, I would take a boat back. Really I would. A boat back to France. Like the first time. The first time, I took the *Queen Mary*. I was only eighteen then. I had never been anywhere except to New Orleans, and, oh, yes, I had been to Nag's Head. Nag's Head, North Carolina, was where I went to visit Amy— Amy, I told you, didn't I, was my best friend? And Amy's parents owned a house in Nag's Head. I love the ocean and I love to swim, Lily. I swim here in Old Saybrook, only now it's raining. It's been raining all week and the water here is much colder than the water off the coast—oh, and I just thought of this—Inez—Inez did not know how to swim. Did you know this, Lily? When Price told me I could not believe this either. Everyone knows how to swim was what I said to him."

I said, "Of course, I know how to swim. My mother taught me how to swim when I was little, but my father—my father, Molly, always said he had a healthy respect for the ocean."

Molly said, "And I asked Price: How come Inez did not know how to swim? How come Inez graduated from high school without passing the test? Inez, Price said, knew how to tread water and anyway, you did not have to pass the test to graduate from high school then. You only had to pass the test later and to graduate from college. Inez, Price said, only went to college after, while he himself, Price said, did not go to college ever. After Price was discharged from the Navy, he went to art school, he said. Just think, Lily—Price a sailor? Can you picture Price in those pants? And Price said he was stationed in Norfolk, and Norfolk, Lily, is not far from Nag's Head. But I was already in France by then—I had already met Matisse by then. How old is Price Junior? Norfolk was where Inez said Price Junior was born. And what was it Inez said? With Price Junior, Inez said she was in labor for thirty-six hours and still she was not dilated enough. Oh, and on the roof and when Inez was sunbathing nude—and how I was just telling you, Lily—right away, I remember, I noticed the scar. The scar was unusually large—a jagged scar. Too bad, and in France, Lily—the south of France where I met Matisse and where I went swimming, Lily—I saw dozens of women in tiny little string bikinis with barely a pencil mark. Inez's skin, maybe. Inez had very fine skin. Thin skin. The kind of skin you feel you can see through. Inez's skin and Inez's hair—don't you agree, Lily?—were by far Inez's best features. Inez was lucky, too. Inez hardly had any wrinkles, any wrinkles to speak of, or if you compared Inez, Lily, to someone say, like myself. I am just a few years older than Inez and I have plenty of wrinkles already—have you taken a look at my neck recently?"

I said, "Inez was my age, Molly, only I was born in October."

Molly said, "Only if you looked closely, Lily, or if you looked at Inez in the bright light or outdoors in the sunshine, then you could see these little blue veins on Inez's forehead. A whole network of them. The same little blue veins showed up again under Inez's eyes and on the sides of her chin. And those little veins—capillaries, I guess—made Inez seem fragile somehow. Those little veins too, made me think that Inez did not grow up in Wisconsin the way Inez said she had and that Inez grew up somewhere indoors—somewhere airless and crowded. And Inez was not exactly what I would call the athletic type. But Inez did surprise me. Inez surprised me the time we went riding. Have I told you, Lily? I told Nora. I told Nora how Inez rode this big horse. The horse, I swear, Lily, was over seventeen hands high, which just goes to show what I have always said: The bigger the horse, the gentler he is."

I said, "Just what I have always said too, Molly. Leonard is six feet two."

Molly said, "Small horses tend to be mean—like when I was a child in Virginia, in Crozet. I had a pony. A pony named Domino. Lily, I swear to you, every time I rode Domino, Domino tried to kill me. Every time too, I complained to my father about Domino—my father, Lily, was a great horseman. My father was Master of the Hounds of Albermarle County. In front of my father, of course, and wouldn't you know it, Domino always acted like he was the best trained horse in the world—ears forward, eyes not rolling. And, of course, too, my father would not believe a word I said about Domino. But at night, I would lie awake in bed and I would try to think up ways of paying Domino back. For instance, I would go for days, Lily, three or four days, not cleaning out Domino's stall. Let Domino stand in his own shit was what I would think. I am telling you, Lily, it got vicious between us. All animals, Lily—like children—are a huge responsibility, and just look at me, if ever we sell this house, this house in Connecticut, I will have to go back to France with the cat. And the cat, Lily, has a way of always disappearing just before we are meant to be leaving, to say nothing of having to fly all the way back to France with the cat clawing his way out of the bag on my lap. But when I said children, Lily, I was also talking about Bibi. Inez's two boys are a lot older, although Inez, I remember, said: No matter, I never stop worrying. Inez said she worried about Price Junior all the way out there in San Francisco with the girl friend—Sara. Sara the dancer. Inez said she also worried about earthquakes, and what else did Inez say she worried about, Lily? Oh, now I remember— the convergence of planets. Everyone, Inez said to me, including the Indians, predicted the world would come to an end then, and Inez said how first she wanted to throw crystals into the Pacific, only Price would not let her. Price told Inez to take a ride on the Staten Island Ferry, to throw her crystals in there, into the Atlantic. It was a whole lot cheaper, was what Price said to Inez. The same weekend. The weekend I started to tell you about, Lily. The weekend Inez went riding after the argument—no, not the argument over the crystals, the argument over Jack Kennedy, over Jackie."

I said, "Jackie? Jackie Kennedy? Jackie Onassis, you mean." Molly said, "Suzanne and Harry were there. So were Fred and Havier. Fred and Havier came after dinner. No, no, Lily, this was not a dinner party. You know me, I hate to cook. Claude-Marie cooks. In France, Claude-Marie does all the cooking. Claude-Marie does the shopping on his way home from the gallery. Claude-Marie likes to do this. Claude-Marie likes to talk to all the people, to all the shopkeepers, to the butcher, the baker, the woman with the goiter on rue Vaugirard who sells Claude-Marie fresh vegetables—well, frankly, I don't think her vegetables are so fresh, but this is not something I am going to get into with you just now—Claude-Marie knows all their names. Claude-Marie knows how many children they all have, and this is the kind of thing I hate. I hate to make small talk. I have no small talk to make. I hate to talk forever about the weather."

I said, "I know what you mean—rain, rain, rain. Is it still raining in Connecticut? They say it is going to rain all week. This was what I am afraid of—afraid it will rain for Leslie's wedding. Leslie's wedding is on Friday, Molly."

Molly said, "Still, I said to Claude-Marie, I can't stay cooped up all day in the house sorting through all these things. I have to go for a walk on the beach, Lily. I am a real beachcomber at heart—no telling what you can find sometimes. I found the shoe horn, didn't I? I found the seagull. I found the seagull after a storm—a hurricane. The beach was full of debris washed up from the sea. What was the name of the hurricane? This was after they stopped being sexist and after they began

naming hurricanes after men. Havier was with me. Havier
was telling me about how grateful he was to AA and about
how if he had not quit drinking, Fred—Carol. Lily, Carol
was the name of that hurricane, and you should see Havier
now, Lily. Havier is a changed person. You would never
recognize Havier now, and Havier helped me put the seagull
into the trunk of the car—the same car. The car we have
now. I was still driving then. This was the year I stayed in
Connecticut alone all winter to photocopy the seagull. Well,
nearly alone. Tom was there. Lily? Lily—are you listening?"
  I said, "Yes, Tom—it's getting late, Molly."
  Molly said, "Tom was supposed to fix the roof—like Kevin.
I mean Kevin could have fixed things. Kevin could have fixed
the refrigerator that was always leaking, Kevin could have
painted the front hall. God knows, there was plenty of fixing
and painting that Kevin could have done, I said to Inez—
only Tom, Tom—I have to admit—did not finish fixing the
roof, Tom did not work out the way I had planned. And, Lily,
I am the first to admit this. I admitted it to Claude-Marie,
Lily. Some old busybody ran into Claude-Marie in the grocery
store—the grocery store that stays open on Sundays—which
is why frankly, I prefer France. In France, this kind of thing
is not so important. In France, I am a foreigner, people leave
me alone. People assume what I do is odd. Different—the
photocopying is what I am talking about now, Lily. From the
very beginning, Lily, when I was still photocopying clothes—
remember? Clothes with double seams, clothes with hand-
stitched button holes. Every time too, I had to go farther and
farther by bus or by metro to other arrondissements from where
I lived on rue Madame. I'll never forget this—everywhere I
went, everyone accused me of stripping the beads. Now, thank
God, I have my own photocopier. The last time, come to

think of it, I had any trouble photocopying something was photocopying Inez's scarf. Poor Inez. I never heard the end of this. Yes—no—Lily, not the scarf in the restaurant with the bangles, the spangles. I have no idea where that ugly scarf came from. If I had to venture a guess, I would guess the scarf came from the second-hand clothing store in Soho where Malcolm bought the plaid cummerbund. Oh, and please, Lily, please, do not ask me why Malcolm bought the cummerbund if that is what you want to know. I have no idea. Not the foggiest notion. Maybe Malcolm bought the cummerbund to take to someone in Africa. Malcolm, don't forget, is always talking about how Africa changed his art—or was it his life? No, his art, and Inez had one of Malcolm's sculptures, a Masai, standing right there behind the couch, and Price told Inez—what was it Price said? Price said to Inez that if she swore never to sell it, sell the Masai, Inez could keep it, and Inez told Price that, of course, she would never sell Malcolm's sculpture but that Price could not tell her what to do with it either. If she, Inez, wanted to sell the Masai, she bloody well could and she would too, which reminds me—did I tell you what Claude-Marie said about Price? Claude-Marie said when all this was finished that Price was going to go to Cincinnati for a show."

I said, "Cincinnati? Cincinnati is awful, Molly. Believe me, Sam and I spent a few months in Cincinnati and, aside from the zoo, there is nothing to do. Hello? Molly? Molly—it is nearly two-thirty in the morning."

Molly said, "Is it that late? Hold on just one more minute—what was I saying? Oh, how Price told Claude-Marie he was going to Cincinnati while Price was watering the gardenia plants—Inez's gardenias—and while Claude-Marie was turning out the lights, and you know what else Claude-Marie said,

Lily? Claude-Marie said, Price looked as if he had fallen into a trance. Price looked a lot older, and the whole time too, while Price was watering the gardenia plants and picking off the dead leaves, Fiddle, Claude-Marie said—oh, Fiddle! Fiddle is her name, Lily! Price's new wife's name! Thank God! I knew all along I would remember Fiddle eventually. And I knew too, the way to remember Fiddle was not to think about it. To think about something else. But, Lily, what can Fiddle possibly stand for? I am asking you, do you know, Lily? Nora might know—she and Fiddle take the same yoga class—but what was I saying? Oh, Fiddle. Fiddle, Claude-Marie said, was asking Price while he was watering the gardenia plants what he was going to do with them. Fiddle was telling Price he could not throw these plants out and he could not keep the plants either, and all the time, according to Claude-Marie, Price was acting as if he could not hear Fiddle—could not hear what Fiddle was saying to him. Price never once answered Fiddle, and Fiddle—I already told you, Lily—was wearing those rubber gloves, and this was when Claude-Marie said to her: No good deed goes unpunished."

I said, "Molly, what? You have to speak into the receiver, I can't hear you again. What did Claude-Marie say to Fiddle?"

Molly said, "No good deed goes unpunished is Claude-Marie's favorite American expression. This and Be careful what you wish for. There is no way, Claude-Marie says, you can translate these expressions into French. In French, Claude-Marie says, these expressions make no sense. Like As I Lay Dying, the Faulkner novel—the classic example of the untranslatable. As a matter of fact, Lily, this is what we talked about in the car. No, not the Faulkner novel—Be careful what you wish for. The time I was telling you about. The time the plane crashed and I told Yuri that lying and wishing were not the same thing. The reason I told Yuri the plane crashed, was that the baggage door blew open. This had nothing to do with me, I said. Anyway, I should know better than to feel guilty and than to listen to Yuri—Yuri is nothing but a superstitious old peasant from Russia. The money too, Lily. The five hundred dollars is what I am thinking about now, and if I had lent Inez the thousand she wanted, Inez would have spent it. Spent the money on Kevin. Spent the money on something. To be honest—to be honest with you, Lily—only I don't like to say this, this is the trouble with lending people money. The five hundred dollars is gone. Gone forever. Most of the time—you know me, Lily—most of the time, I never think about money. Claude-Marie is the one who thinks about money. Claude-Marie thinks about money all the time. When I was young, Lily, I never had any money. Not a centime, Lily. If I had had money then, I would have never done half the things I have done. I would never, for instance, have met the French count. I would never have met Matisse, Lily. Henri Matisse."

I said, "Oh, yes, you told me about meeting Matisse already, Molly."

Molly said, "I was just lucky was what. I was lucky, too, to meet the count. The time I lived with the count in the abandoned razor blade factory was the happiest time in my life. Swear to God, Lily. I never had to do anything, and the count too, was so punctual. Every night at seven o'clock sharp, I heard his car arrive—a Citroën. The kind of car French officials drive. The kind of car that sinks into itself with kind of a relieved groan when it stops. I would watch from the window, Lily, as the count pulled up in front of the abandoned factory door. I would watch as the count took out the packages from the back of the car, packages of paté and wine. I watched how the count would open the hard-to-open door with this large metal key, a key that looked like the key to a medieval city— Lily?"

I said, "Hmmm—yes."

Molly said, "But, Lily, you should have tasted the wine. Wine from the count's own vineyard, a vineyard somewhere near Bordeaux. A vineyard that had belonged to the count's father and to the count's father's father before that. The count said he could trace his ancestry all the way back to before the French Revolution and to Louis the Fourteenth. So could his wife. Isabelle. Isabelle and I are still good friends, Lily. As a matter of fact, Isabelle is how I met Claude-Marie. Through Isabelle's sister."

I said, "Isabelle has a sister? You know what time it is, Molly?"

Molly said, "Oh, God, it's late, I know. We should get off the phone. But I told you, didn't I, about Isabelle's sister? About how Isabelle and her sister met Matisse. A kind of coincidence. I mean Matisse and the French count. No, no, no, don't get me wrong, I didn't sleep with Matisse. Neither did Isabelle. The whole point of the story, Lily, is that when they were children—Isabelle and her sister—their mother was invited to have tea with Matisse and with somebody else, somewhere in the south of France where Isabelle's mother went every summer. While Isabelle's mother was having tea, Isabelle and her sister were playing in the garden and all of a sudden, Matisse came out. Isabelle said she got frightened, so did her sister, frightened Matisse would ask them what they were doing there in his garden. But Matisse just took a pee. Afterwards, Matisse went up to Isabelle and her sister—Isabelle and her sister were about the same height then—and Matisse asked Isabelle if she and her sister were twins."

I said, "Twins? Oh, I think I've heard this story before. I think you've told me this story, Molly, only I can't remember."

Molly said, "But since Isabelle was still frightened and she did not want to contradict Matisse, Isabelle said: Yes, yes—they, she and her sister, were twins. Later—and after she had finished her tea—Isabelle's mother told Isabelle she was curious and she had seen Isabelle through the window outside in the garden talking to Matisse, and what, Isabelle's mother wanted to know, had Matisse said. Since Isabelle did not want to tell her mother that she had lied to Matisse, Isabelle told her mother that Matisse had asked her what her favorite color was. Isabelle told her mother: *Blue.* Isabelle said she had told Matisse blue was her favorite color, and Matisse, Isabelle said, had told her, blue, was his, too. And from then on, Isabelle's mother went around telling everyone that she knew for certain what Matisse's favorite color was. But what I like best about this story, Lily, is that blue was probably Matisse's favorite color all along. Blue is the most popular color. Yellow is the least. Yellow is the most difficult and someone—oh, yes, I know—it was Inez. Inez said yellow was supposed to give you an appetite. This was why the insides of restaurants were painted yellow. So were the tablecloths and the napkins yellow. But when Price overheard Inez say this—this was right here in Old Saybrook, Lily—Price shouted across the table at Inez: *What about van Gogh, Inez? Van Gogh's sunflowers do not make me hungry. Van Gogh's sunflowers are tragic.* I'll never forget this—the way Price shouted. The way I'll never forget Price in Paris, Lily. Price in his plaid jacket. Price on the Boulevard Montparnasse, Price climbing to the top of the Eiffel Tower. Good exercise, he said. Price ran—remember? Price ran a marathon. He ran the time the woman took the subway and cheated—I forget her name. Inez would know. I know

37

Inez would remember. The woman's name was just the kind of thing Inez would remember. The way Inez could remember birthdays. Not just birthdays of relatives. Inez could remember Natalie Wood's birthday—October eleventh. Inez also used to cut out clippings from newspapers and magazines. Inez would send them to me. Those clippings must be around here somewhere—somewhere in with the interview probably, and in with the coupon for a free meal and cocktail. Here! Oh, Lily, isn't this amazing? Isn't this a coincidence? Swear to God—right here—I found one of the clippings Inez sent me. You won't believe this. Lily, this is the one about a woman who found a live hand grenade in her bag of potatoes and the woman—wait, I am rereading this—the woman lived in Neuilly, which was why, I guess, Inez—oh, and Neuilly is right on the other side of the Bois de Boulogne, Lily. But Claude-Marie—this is what I told Inez—Claude-Marie does all the shopping and anyway, Claude-Marie does not eat potatoes any more. Brussels sprouts, too. Claude-Marie does not eat brussels sprouts either any more on account of the war. And it makes no difference, Lily, that I have told Claude-Marie that the war was over forty years ago and that he was only a small boy then, and I have told you, Lily, haven't I, how Claude-Marie is not always practical? As a matter of fact, just now, I told Claude-Marie since he had to drive all the way to the morgue, he might as well kill two birds with one stone and buy himself an airline ticket. Only I said: Claude-Marie, please, for God's sakes, don't buy a ticket on Air India."

I said, "Air India? What's wrong with Air India? I've flown Air India. The food on Air India is delicious. They serve curry—oh. Was it Air India that crashed, Molly, while you were in the car with Yuri and Price?"

Molly said, "Bibi too. Don't forget, Lily, Bibi was in the

car, and, no, it was British Airways. A DC-10 Airbus. I never saw so much smoke in my life. On the highway, the cars had to turn on their headlights. This was right in the middle of the day—around noon, I would say. We had not had lunch yet. Lunch was what Claude-Marie and I had argued about and why I told Claude-Marie to call his sister, Dominique, and tell her we had had an accident. I had also told Bibi she could look at the horses. The horses at Chantilly, and while Bibi was looking at the horses, I had told Yuri he could go over to the chateau and look at the book of hours—the famous book of hours of the duke of Something-Somebody-or-other. At the time, Lily, I did not realize they no longer exhibited the real book of hours, they exhibited a facsimile. Anyhow. As it turned out, none of this mattered. Claude-Marie turned the car right around and we drove back to Paris. I remember, Price said he was just as glad. No, not glad about the plane crash, glad about going back to Paris. Since this was his last day, Price said he wanted to take another look at Notre Dame. I said I would go with him. No—you know me, Lily, I am not religious, and Price is a Quaker. I just like to sit and listen to the music. The organ music, and the one real regret I have in my whole life besides the French count is that I cannot play an instrument. Why I make Bibi take piano lessons. Piano lessons from Mademoiselle Boudemange. Oh, and did I tell you this? Did I tell you, Lily, that Mademoiselle Boudemange said she knew Artur Rubinstein? As a matter of fact, Mademoiselle Boudemange said that Artur Rubinstein gave her a piano—a Bechstein. But the Bechstein is not the piano Bibi practices on. Mademoiselle Boudemange won't let her. No. Bibi practices on a Yamaha."

I said, "A Yamaha? I thought a Yamaha was a motorcycle, Molly."

Molly said, "Lily, the only thing I know about motorcycles is that Jerome has one, which is another reason why I worry about Bibi. I told you, Dominique is in the real estate business and Dominique is away all day in her car, and who, I ask you, is looking after Bibi? The fat Portuguese babysitter and Jerome? Jerome is Dominique's adopted son, and who knows what Jerome is up to right now. Jerome and Véronique— Véronique is Jerome's sister—I do not trust either one of these adopted children, which was why I told Claude-Marie—after he identified Inez at the morgue—to go buy the ticket, but Claude-Marie said tomorrow. By the time he had finished, the airline office, Claude-Marie said, would be closed. Oh— I forgot to tell Claude-Marie about the car. I forgot to tell Claude-Marie that today is Wednesday if it is alternate parking. I'll always remember, Lily, how when I was first married I used to sit in the car for two hours and read the newspaper. I have never been so well informed in my life. I read the sports page, I read the stock market report, I even read the obituaries. You would be surprised too, Lily, at how much you can learn from the obituaries. Really, I am not kidding, which reminds me, at Harvard, Claude-Marie—Claude-Marie, you know, Lily, went to the Harvard Business School. A lot of Frenchmen do. Harvard is the only American school Frenchmen have heard of. But what was I saying? Oh, I know, Claude-Marie had a professor who told his students that the only thing they needed to read to pass his course were the obituaries. Frankly, I am not sure Harvard did Claude-Marie much good, and I am not even going to mention that crook again, Thomas Hamlin Aldrich. He went to the Harvard Business School too, Lily. This was where Claude-Marie met him. One thing I do know, I am not going to go to Claude-Marie's twenty-fifth reunion with him. I never went to my own—my own high school reunion. The only person I want to see again is Amy. And I do see Amy anyway. I see Amy at funerals. Charlie, too. Only Charlie was not in my class at high school. Charlie was a freshman at UVA. Charlie, Lily, was the one who caused all that ruckus by putting the raven inside Edgar Allan Poe's room, and he was the one about whom the man from the S.P.C.A. said: People like Charlie should be locked up. Oh, but what time did you say it was now? It's too late, I guess, to call Claude-Marie about the alternate parking. But what was I saying? Charlie? The funny thing, Lily, is that Charlie *is* locked up, only Charlie is locked up for a different reason. It is too late, isn't it? I would hate to wake up Nora. Nora works hard, and I have always said that a simultaneous translator at the United Nations has a huge responsibility. This is what I tell Bibi, Lily."

I said, "Molly, you took the words right out of my mouth —speaking another language is a big asset. Have I told you yet how I have joined a French conversation club?"

Molly said, "Me, too—first thing I did was to take French lessons. And luckily Matisse spoke a little English. Otherwise, I would not have understood a word Matisse said, which was what I said to Havier. Havier speaks fluent Spanish. Price, too, is a good example. French would have come in handy the time Price wanted to buy Inez a souvenir and I said: Get her perfume or get her a scarf—and Claude-Marie was right. Claude-Marie was right when he said that Price had made money by selling a sculpture and that Price felt guilty for not bringing Inez to Paris, and the reason I remember this so vividly, Lily, was that this was during dinner and I had just told Claude-Marie how Price and I had had the drink on Boulevard Montparnasse, and Claude-Marie said: Too bad, too, about Inez. Too bad Inez did not come to Paris with

Price, and I said to Claude-Marie: Too bad about whom? Who is this Inez anyhow that you are talking about? All this was while we were eating the tart, Lily. I swear to you, and Claude-Marie, I remember, said how he had bought the lemon tart from Madame Florisson on rue du Bac. Claude-Marie said how although it was a Sunday, the bakery was open, and Claude-Marie said how he had talked to Madame Florisson —no—Madame Florisson, Lily, is not the woman with the goiter, Madame Florisson is the woman with the daughter-in-law. And according to Claude-Marie, Madame Florisson's daughter-in-law had just arrived from Nantes the day before because the next day, Monday—and Monday, Claude-Marie also said, the bakery would be closed—the daughter-in-law had an appointment to see a specialist about her kidneys, and Bibi, who was at the table with us, asked me where the kidneys were. I told Bibi I had no idea. I told Bibi, I did not have the foggiest notion. I still don't."

I said, "I always get where the kidneys and the liver are mixed up."

Molly said, "The lemon tart, too, was delicious and you cannot find a lemon tart like this in Connecticut, but what was I saying? Oh, Price—Price wanted to buy Inez something. Men, too, Lily, are funny this way—I am speaking of presents. Take Claude-Marie. Claude-Marie gave up after the red sweater. The red sweater Claude-Marie gave me was definitely the wrong kind of red. Except for someone like Inez. Inez was someone who could get away with wearing red. Inez wore a red wool dress in Old Saybrook the time Suzanne and Harry came for dinner and the time I was telling you about when we argued about the crystals and Jackie Kennedy. Oh, and after dinner, I remember, Inez spoke Spanish to Havier. Funny the things you remember. At first, Inez said she could not remember any—any Spanish that is—but once she started to talk to Havier, Spanish, Inez said, came back to her and—oh, Lily, I'll never forget this either—it was strange too, to hear Inez talk in another language. In another language, Inez looked more animated. And it was funny how Price said he did not remember any Spanish. Price said he did not remember as much Spanish as Inez did, and Inez said this was because Price was always locked up in his studio, while she, Inez, was out doing the marketing and talking to all the people, and Price said as far as he was concerned, Spain was a mistake, and Price was probably thinking of the boy Jesus. Of Jesus Ramirez. I told you, Lily, how Price told Fiddle the water was running and he had walked in on them. Anyway—or, so Nora said. Only I don't believe everything Nora says. I don't believe what Nora said about Mercedes, her sister, and I don't believe what Nora said about Yuri and all the women on her sofa bed—the same sofa bed Claude-Marie is sleeping on right this minute, Lily—oh, and the lobsters. Did you hear about the lobsters, Lily? This is funny, because last year, when Yuri came to New York for his show, the plane—the Air India plane—instead of landing in New York the way it was supposed to, the plane landed in Bangor, Maine. Poor Yuri, Lily. Yuri had to clear customs in Bangor, and while Yuri was waiting to reboard the plane, Yuri bought the lobsters. Yuri said he bought the lobsters to bring to Ivan and Nora as a kind of house present and as a thank-you for letting him sleep on their sofa bed. Yuri also said he told Nora what the woman at the Bangor airport who had sold him the lobsters had said. The woman told Yuri that he had to cook the lobsters alive in boiling water."

I said, "I know, Molly. Everyone knows this—the water has to come to a rolling boil."

Molly said, "Only neither Ivan nor Yuri would do it, Lily

—boil the lobsters alive, I mean. They told Nora that they were Russian and that they couldn't possibly. Nora had to. I tell you, Lily, Yuri got away with murder in New York. In New York, there is a whole network of Russians: Russian waiters, Russian poets, Russian taxicab drivers—Inez's cab driver, remember? The cab driver Inez said *fuck you* to, the day we had lunch, the same day Inez asked me for the money—and you know what I keep thinking, Lily? I keep thinking five hundred dollars is a lot of money. I keep thinking you can do a lot with five hundred dollars—my Leica, for example. I sold Yuri my Leica for five hundred dollars but Yuri has only paid me for half of it. Yuri still owes me two hundred and fifty dollars. The last time I reminded Yuri about the Leica, Yuri said—and you know how Yuri talks: 'I give beautiful painting to you Mow-li instead.' What could I say, Lily? I don't want one of Yuri's paintings. Yuri paints legless chairs. I want my money. My two hundred and fifty dollars. It was a good camera, Lily. The camera I took the pictures of Isabelle and the French count with for the magazine. Funny, how things work out, isn't it? Just because I took that picture of Matisse, everyone assumed I was a professional photographer. Beginner's luck, because to tell you the truth, Lily, I didn't know the first thing about photography. If someone talked to me about F-stops, I swear, Lily, I started to feel sick to my stomach. Believe me, photocopying is a lot easier. A photocopying artist is more like a technician. I have never met another photocopying artist. I just met one once—a woman. She photocopied her backside, her naked backside—I promise you—at all different hours. 'Ass at Noon,' 'Ass at Night' was how she titled her art. I hate people like this, don't you, Lily? They give photocopying a bad name. It is bad enough now that everyone photocopies their hands. They photocopy newborn babies' feet too. When Bibi was born, all they did was put little beads around Bibi's wrist that spelled out my last name, only I remember they misspelled it. I didn't care. I told the nurse: As long as it's my baby and I am not like—oh, but Inez—remember Inez, Lily? Remember how Inez was touchy about this? About her name—Inez. How Inez had to be spelled with a Z and not with an S. I told Inez I didn't think it made a whole lot of difference. I told Inez what's the difference as long as 'Inez' and 'Ines' are pronounced the same, only Inez did not see it this way. Inez said she could never identify herself with an S. I said: But Inez, you are so lucky. Inez is a name that sounds good in all different languages. Take Molly, for instance. In French, Molly sounds terrible."

I said, "Inez is a Spanish name, isn't it? Don Juan's mother's name was Inez. Who else was there? There was an Inez de Castro."

Molly said, "Who? Don Juan? Oh, don't ask me why I just thought of this, Lily. I just did. Price is a Quaker, and I'll never forget how Inez said when she first met Price's family and she had to have lunch with them. Before lunch, before they started to eat, and instead of saying grace, Inez said how they had to have a moment of silence at the same time that they all had to hold hands around the dining room table. Inez said how there she was holding hands with Price's mother and Price's father and there she was two months pregnant already and she started to laugh. Ha, ha, ha. I know all about inappropriate laughter, Lily. The same thing happened to me in church at the count's funeral. In France. Thank God, there was a lot of loud music and singing and I was not sitting up in front with Isabelle and her sister and with the rest of the family. I was sitting in the back with the maid and the cook. The gardener was there too. His name was Lucien, and Lu-

cien, I remember, was a very old man, and Lucien told everyone how he could remember the war of—what was it?—the
war of eighteen something, Lily. The war when the Russians
occupied Paris. Anyhow, this isn't important—what I remember is how Lucien said that when the Russian soldiers went
to eat at the French restaurants, they would bang their fists
on the table at the same time that they would shout out to the
waiters: *Bistro, bistro!* which means 'hurry' in Russian and the
name stuck. The other thing that happened was that I was the
only woman in church not wearing a hat. Can you imagine?
Everyone in Paris wore a hat to a funeral. I haven't worn a
hat in I don't know how long. I didn't wear a hat to my own
father's funeral. You know why? I had to wear a hat to school.
It was part of the uniform. One time, I'll never forget this, I
threw my hat into the river—just a small river, the Rivanna
River—and the next day, wouldn't you know, some boy found
the hat floating in the water. He brought it back to me. The
hat had my name sewn into the brim. To make matters worse,
my mother said I was lucky they did not have to drag the river
for me and I should give the boy something, a part of my
allowance, she said—speaking of which, speaking of money.
Price told Claude-Marie he wanted to give the delivery boy
something. A reward. The delivery boy, Claude-Marie said,
nearly lost his job for delivering the wrong tuxedo, and thank
God, too, was what Price said. Thank God, Fiddle did not
throw out the tuxedo with the rest of Kevin's stuff—the condoms and the T-shirts—although what I told Claude-Marie
was, dry-cleaners are insured. I told Claude-Marie the second
time he called. I told Claude-Marie: Remember the time the
dry-cleaner lost your favorite jacket? The tweed Italian sports
jacket? Claude-Marie said he was calling from Nora and Ivan's
apartment then, only Nora, Claude-Marie said, was not home

46

yet. Only Ivan was home, and Ivan told Claude-Marie that Nora had had to go to a formal black-tie dinner at the Waldorf Astoria. Poor Nora. Nora said it was almost impossible for her to both eat her dinner and to translate. Nora said, the last time she went to a formal dinner she nearly choked to death on her entrée."

I said, "Oh, the same thing happened to my father and if the waiter had not been standing behind him, my father, I promise you, Molly, would have died right then and there."

Molly said, "Yes, Nora was lucky, and one time, I asked Nora: Nora, tell me—when you finally get to bed, what language do you dream in? I told Nora Claude-Marie speaks French to me if he is saying something like: *Chérie, je t'aime*—oh, this reminds me of this silly joke about what an asset speaking two languages is, the joke Ivan told us. Most of the time I don't remember jokes, but don't worry, Lily, this joke is not dirty—this joke is not like the other one, like the one about the horse's dick—remember? This one is about how the King of Norway goes on a stag hunt and how at the end of the day and after the King of Norway has shot hundreds of stags, this man comes running out of the forest with his arms up in the air and says: Don't shoot me, King, I am *not* a stag. And the King of Norway shoots him anyway. Ivan told us this joke the time he and Nora came for the weekend—the day I ran over the cat, the day Nora lost her suitcase, the same day that Inez phoned to say she had found someone to rent her room to—Kevin. Only, I was not home then, I was having a cup of coffee at Alicia Thomas's house. Inez spoke to Claude-Marie. Claude-Marie said, on the phone, Inez asked him if he knew where LeGrange, Texas, was, and Claude-Marie told Inez he had only been to Texas the once. To Dallas and to Fort Worth. And Claude-Marie said he told Inez: But the

new museum in Forth Worth—in his opinion anyway—was the best small museum in the world. The lighting
was what Claude-Marie said he told Inez he meant. Also,
Claude-Marie was distracted. The whole time Claude-Marie
said he was talking to Inez, Claude-Marie was also wondering
where I was. Claude-Marie had seen the car in the driveway
—I don't know whether Claude-Marie had seen the fender
yet—and Nora and Ivan were standing around in the front
hall holding their suitcases—oh, except Nora was not. I told
you how Nora had lost her suitcase on Amtrak—the same
train I lost Inez's scarf on—the scarf Inez was knitting for
Price. But what was I saying? Oh, the whole time Claude-
Marie was talking to Inez on the phone—Claude-Marie, of
course, knew all about the divorce and all about Price and
Fiddle and how they were going to get married in February,
and Claude-Marie had said over and over again how he just
did not want to get in the middle—the whole time, too, when
he was on the phone with Inez, Nora, Claude-Marie said, was
nattering away about her darn suitcase. Nora said her suitcase
was right there in the overhead rack. Right there, too, above
her head for the entire journey to Old Saybrook. Nora said
she never left her seat except for the once to go to the bathroom.
Ivan and Claude-Marie never left their seats either. The lost
suitcase was a complete mystery. I had to lend Nora a night-
gown and Nora talked about her lost suitcase and what was in
it nonstop all weekend. You should have heard her, Lily. Nora
even called up the railroad. She threatened to sue them,
she said, for the brand-new cashmere sweater set she had never
worn yet. On the phone, the man from Amtrak laughed.
First he told Nora, Nora had to prove negligence. Harry—
Suzanne's husband—is a lawyer, a litigator, although you
would never know it, Lily. Harry is so soft-spoken. Suzanne

is the one who has the loud voice. Harry told Nora that negligence is difficult to prove and, to prove his point, Harry told Nora the story of Churchill and the radio—God, Lily, even if I have heard Harry tell this story a dozen times, this is one of the worst stories I have ever heard—hello? Hello, Lily?"

I said, "Hello—yes, Harry's story, I forget."

Molly said, "I first heard the story years ago and right after Harry and Suzanne had sailed alone across the Atlantic in Harry's new sailboat—a ketch—and Suzanne stopped smoking. Oh—this is true too, Lily, have you heard this? Suzanne said that somewhere in the middle of the Atlantic, a whale started to follow them, follow the boat—the ketch. Although the whale was just playing, Suzanne said—the whale kept diving and surfacing on either side of the ketch—still, with a flip of its tail, Suzanne said, the whale could have capsized the ketch. This went on for hours and Suzanne got so frightened, she said, she got so anxious, that she promised God she would do anything if God would only make the whale swim away. Suzanne said she threw her two cartons of Marlboros overboard. For good measure, she also threw over the gold Cartier lighter Harry had given her for their fifteenth wedding anniversary. Later, however, and according to Suzanne, Harry said throwing the lighter into the ocean had been unnecessary. Suzanne said she told Harry that no, she associated the lighter with a bad habit and not with their marriage—oh, speaking of bad marriages, this reminds me of another story, Lily. Were you there? Were you there in East Hampton when Malcolm told us about this woman he had met in an ashram, an Indian woman who was enlightened named Ananda Somebody-or-other, and each time Ananda's husband tried to make love to her, to Ananda, he—the husband, Lily—got a tremendous electric shock. I don't know why I mention this now—ha, ha—only Inez, too, I remember, got a kick out of this story. Inez told Malcolm this was one sure method of contraception and much more fun than sticking your fork inside a toaster."

I said, "Molly, will you hold on for a minute? I'm going to get myself something to drink. I'll pick up the phone in the kitchen."

Molly said, "Oh, yes, of course, yes. What time is it, Lily?"

I said, "Hello, Molly. I'm here. I'm in the kitchen. I am going to make myself some cocoa. There is nothing like a good cup of cocoa on a night like this."

Molly said, "I am drinking tea, Lily. My tea is probably cold by now, Lily, but what was I saying?"

I said, "Molly, I am heating the milk. It must be almost three o'clock in the morning, Molly."

Molly said, "Hello—has it stopped raining? Has it stopped raining in New York yet? It has rained all week in Connecticut and each time, I ask Bibi on the phone about whether it's raining in France, Bibi says she doesn't know—but what was I saying, what was I talking about? Oh, *Inez.* I was talking about Inez, Lily, and how the skin inside Inez's arm—did you ever notice this, Lily?—was slightly discolored, a little brownish. This happened while Price was still in the Navy, Inez said, while he and Inez were living in Norfolk, and the doctor told Inez it was her decision, and you know what I told Inez? I told Inez: Who is he fooling? Skin grafts are painful. Skin grafts are not like implants. I told Inez to just take a look at my mother, for example. My mother, I told Inez—the time I flew from Paris on one day's notice and my mother was in the Martha Jefferson Hospital—had to have cataract surgery, and you know what the ophthalmologist told *me?* The ophthalmologist told me the lens he was putting in my mother's eye was made out of plastic—the same kind of plastic bomber

windshields are made out of—but no, wait, not because the
plastic bomber windshields don't break—no. On the contrary
was what the ophthalmologist said, because if the bomber
windshields do break and if the plastic does fly into the pilots'
eyes, the pilots do not reject it. The other thing the ophthalmologist told me was that cataracts are genetic, but I am not
going to worry about this yet. First, I have to have a root canal.
Oh, and remember Matisse, Lily? Matisse could hardly see a
thing either. And Matisse, I'll never forget, was such a gen-
tleman—this was before I had had my hair cut, Lily—Matisse
was so complimentary. Matisse, too, kept right on painting
from his wheelchair until the very end, Lily. Degas, too, was
almost blind. So was Monet. Musicians maybe go deaf—oh,
Claude-Marie, Lily. Either Claude-Marie is losing his hearing
or Claude-Marie does not listen—like the parking, Lily. I told
Claude-Marie: Don't forget, unless you want to get a ticket.
Oh, I almost forgot—forgot, Lily, what I started to tell you.
The day Inez phoned about Kevin and Claude-Marie answered
the phone, *Claude-Marie* forgot. Because of the car, the cat,
and Nora's lost suitcase, Claude-Marie said he completely
forgot. Claude-Marie only remembered to tell me later, during
dinner and while Ivan, in that funny accent of his, was telling
us the King of Norway on a stag hunt joke, and what Claude-
Marie said then was if he had understood Inez correctly, Kevin
was from Fort Worth—Forth Worth, Texas—and Kevin, Inez
also had said to him, was involved in the new museum. All
of which goes to show you, Lily, how quickly things can get
distorted."

I said, "Wait, the milk for the cocoa is boiling. Hello? What
did you say? If you ask me, it is not how old you are, it is how
old you feel that matters. Leonard is going to be forty-six this
month, Molly."

Molly said, "You are so right, Lily, and I told Inez the same

51

thing. I told Inez: Just because Kevin is a lot younger and just because Kevin was in one commercial once does not mean Kevin is a talented actor. Oh, did you see it, Lily? The commercial for coffee? I saw it by accident. Nora and I were watching a program on the Kalahari Desert when all of a sudden, there was Kevin smacking his lips and saying this coffee tastes delicious, and Nora said if she were to bet, this was just about sex, and I told Nora about how each time now I went over to Inez's and how on my way to the bathroom if the door was open, the door to Inez's bedroom, I mean, and Inez's bed was unmade—and you know how Kevin kept odd hours, how he slept late—I could still tell, Lily, the way you always can, that Inez's bed had not just been slept in, that Inez's bed had been made love in—oh, only Claude-Marie now, and while Price was watering the gardenia plants, Claude-Marie said Inez's bedroom was immaculate. When he went in there to turn off the lights, Inez's bedroom, Claude-Marie said, looked as if it had just been vacuumed. Claude-Marie should know. You should see Claude-Marie, Lily. Claude-Marie is so tidy. I am not. Claude-Marie says if I am in a room for more than five minutes, the room looks as if a cyclone had hit it. This reminds me—remember, Lily? This is funny, this always makes me laugh—when Malcolm's apartment in New York was broken into and Malcolm's neighbors called Malcolm in East Hampton to tell him about it, the neighbors said how sorry they were and they also said that since the thieves had left Malcolm's apartment in such a terrible mess, with Malcolm's things, with Malcolm's clothes all over the floor, it was impossible for them to assess his actual loss. Well, as it turned out, an old TV and a cheap radio were the only things the thieves had stolen. The apartment was just the way Malcolm had left it—*very very* messy. But Claude-Marie hangs up his ties according to color—red ties, gray ones, navy-blue. His shoes too are all lined up. Black, brown, suede. Claude-Marie never leaves anything lying around. Claude-Marie, if he has to, will press his own clothes, sew on his own shirt buttons. Some men, I know, actually like to sew and do delicate needlework. They claim it relaxes them—oh, like Inez's doctor, her obstetrician. Did Inez tell you about him? No, not the first one, the other one—the doctor who delivered the second boy, Matthew. Inez said how this doctor made lace while the women were in labor and while he waited for them—except not with Matthew. Matthew was born so fast the doctor did not even have time to thread his bobbin. Inez told me she woke up in the middle of the night and it was while she and Price were living in Cleveland, and Inez told me how she hated Cleveland, and how even Lake Erie, Inez said, looked dreary to her, and Inez said where they were living, their neighbors had a cat and the cat must have been in heat. Every night, the cat yowled outside their window and when Inez woke up in the middle of the night that night, at first, Inez said, she thought she woke up on account of the cat. Price woke up too, she said. Price got out of bed, and Price told Inez that this time he was going to get rid of this cat once and for good. Inez said she heard Price go get his gun out of the hall closet—a twelve-gauge. Sometimes Price went duck hunting, and Inez heard the screen door slam shut before she realized, she said, that she was in labor. Inez said the contractions were so close together she hardly had the time to time them and she could hardly get out of bed or go to the bathroom. All she could do was yell out of the window to Price to never mind what he was doing now and to come back inside and take her straight to the hospital. Price answered I-nez: Wait, first I have to kill the cat. Inez said her water broke the same instant Price fired the gun."

I said, "Oh."

Molly said, "After this, Inez told me, no more babies, and
I don't blame her. Frankly, I blame Price. I blame Price for
shooting the cat. I know a lot of men like this, and you would
be surprised, Lily—someone like Claude-Marie—Claude-
Marie whom you would never suspect. But if Claude-Marie
ever gets angry, if Claude-Marie ever loses his temper, you
would never know Claude-Marie was the same man. One
time, Claude-Marie got so angry—no, not over Tom—
Claude-Marie threw the kitchen table and knocked a hole in
the ceiling. I swear. I'll never forget this. I just stood there.
I couldn't speak. The table was heavy. The table was solid
oak and it was full of dishes. I had no idea Claude-Marie
could even lift it."

I said, "Sam, too. Didn't I tell you how Sam threw my ring
out of the window? Oh, good, this cocoa is delicious."

Molly said, "People certainly are unpredictable, and Price,
Claude-Marie said, was already shouting at Fiddle—how long
have Price and Fiddle been married? Three months? Claude-
Marie said Fiddle made a remark in passing about the price
tag—how the price tag was still attached to the coat—and
Price said since the coat was brand new, the coat had never
even been worn, he was going to send Inez's new coat to
Patricia, to Inez's sister, and Fiddle told Price this was ridiculous. Of course, Fiddle was right. Hawaii is too hot, San
Francisco is a lot cooler, but Price Junior said anyhow, Sara,
his girlfriend, was allergic to down, and he would rather take
the appliances—the Cuisinart, the machine to make pasta,
the espresso machine. The stereo. Can you believe this, Lily?
Already, they are arguing and I should have told Claude-Marie
to tell Price: If no one wants that damn down coat, I'll take
it. Did I tell you this? The coat was hanging right there on
the coat rack—the coat rack with the umbrellas and hats as

you stepped out of the elevator. Inez, Claude-Marie said, was standing on the other side. Claude-Marie said the police drew in those chalk marks —but the coat is reversible: black on the one side and a yellow leopard spot pattern on the other. I don't care as long as it keeps me warm. I am still wearing the coat Isabelle gave me."

I said, "Molly, I am sure the stereo belonged to Kevin and I told you how when Sam and I got divorced, we argued over everything. We argued over this kettle. This kettle right here on this stove, Molly."

Molly said, "Don't you remember? The coat was how I met you, Lily. In the stationery store. The stationery store right off Boulevard St. Germain. You were in line behind me waiting to photocopy something."

I said, "Oh, yes, a tax form."

Molly said, "That's right, a tax form. Oh, God, but don't mention taxes to me, Lily. I am going through my desk right this minute and I am throwing out all these papers and bills. But what was I saying? The fur coat. I was going to photocopy the fur coat. The coat is that old, Lily. Older—first, the coat belonged to Isabelle. But if Inez's down coat is too big—Inez was a couple of inches taller than me—I can give the coat to Bibi. Bibi is growing so—oh, I was not going to mention this, but did you notice, Lily, how Inez had bought herself all these new clothes recently? And did you notice how Inez said she wanted to redecorate, and I said: Where are all the photos, Inez? The photos of the children? The photo of Price Junior wearing his mortar board and holding his diploma that used to be right here on the coffee table next to the couch—the couch Inez said she wanted to throw out."

I said, "I liked the couch. The couch was unique, Molly."

Molly said, "Listen, I said to Inez, there is nothing wrong

with being over forty. Look at me. Look at Colette, I said. The trouble was the kids, Inez said. The kids were too judgmental. The kids had never met Kevin, and already Price Junior, according to what Fiddle told Nora, had telephoned Price. Price Junior had telephoned at all hours of the night and of the morning on account of the three-hour time difference, and Nora said she was repeating verbatim what she had heard and in Fiddle's very own words: This kid has a real instinct. Every time this kid telephones us we are in bed making love and each time, when I pick up the phone, I have to make my voice sound normal. Fiddle wants babies was the other thing Nora said. Fiddle, come to think of it, Lily, is built just like Dominique, Claude-Marie's sister—small waist, wide hips. Only Dominique cannot have babies. Unless, of course, it is Didier. Didier is Dominique's husband. Didier is the one I no longer speak to. Didier is the one who yelled at me over the Penny Black or whatever the stamp is called, but what I wanted to say was about the babies—the children, the adopted children, Jerome and Véronique. Jerome and Véronique look exactly like Dominique. Maybe it is the food they eat. The same food. Or the climate. In Senlis, it rains all the time. In Chantilly, it is different. Chantilly, remember, was where I wanted to go for lunch the day the plane crashed. Chantilly was where the French count had a weekend house and where Isabelle goes riding. Isabelle is a great horsewoman just like my father was—a great horseman, I mean—which was what I was thinking the day I took the pictures of her for *Marie-Claire*, the magazine. Afterwards, the French count drove me back to Paris in his Lancia. This was how it started, Lily."

I said, "I thought you said the French count owned a Citroën, Molly."

Molly said, "The count owned two cars. The Citroën was

roomier, he left the Citroën in the country for Isabelle. The
French count had a passion for cars, Lily, and the French
count always drove fast, which is ironic, and now, of course,
I don't drive any more. Fred is going to have to drive me to
New London on Thursday. I told you, didn't I, how I had to
have a root canal? The dentist is costing me a small fortune,
and if only I still had the five hundred dollars, the five hundred
dollars I lent to Inez, I would sleep a lot better at nights."

I said, "Maybe I should take my hot cocoa back to bed.
Hello? Molly, are you there? I am just thinking out loud now,
thinking about poor Inez's mother."

Molly said, "No, no. Inez's mother is married to a what-
do-you-call-it rich CEO. There was a whole article in *Fortune*
magazine about his company. Inez's mother's husband's company makes something out of fiberglass for nuclear reactors,
and I told Claude-Marie—I told Claude-Marie a long time
ago and when Thomas Hamlin Aldrich was still alive and still
investing Claude-Marie's money—Claude-Marie should in-
vest in Inez's mother's second husband's company, but what
do I know except I was right, of course. I was right too, when
I asked Inez in the restaurant why she was asking me and not
asking her own flesh and blood, and Inez said, Patricia. Sibling
rivalry. Lily, I should have guessed. Ever since Patricia won
the bronze medal at the Olympics in Rome—Rome, Italy—
ever since the accident in the carriage in Anacapri—have you
been to Anacapri, Lily? It's pretty—flowers, olive trees, ter-
raced hillsides—and Inez told me all the gory details. How
the horse's reins got caught in the bougainvillea, how the
carriage turned over, how the young man Patricia had met
over there—what was his name? An Italian name—I forget
—how he and Patricia were on their way to visit Axel Munthe's
house—oh, this was something else I told Inez. I said: You

won't believe this, Inez. I haven't thought of Axel Munthe in years. My mother used to keep Axel Munthe's book by the side of her bed. The book, I will never forget, had a pale green cover. This was a book my mother claimed had changed her life. When I tried to read it, Lily, I could never get past page ten. Funny too, when you think about this—the kind of things people claim have changed their lives. I knew a man once who said he was struck by lightning while he was horseback riding—no, not Charlie. This is a true story, Lily, this is not a joke. The man said he fell off his horse and wet his pants. He also said I was making too much out of the lightning, but to go back to Patricia—"

I said, "Just a minute, Molly, you are mixing me up. Is the man who was struck by lightning while he was horseback riding the same man who said he had not slept with his wife since the astronauts landed?"

Molly said, "No, no, this man's name was John, Lily—but you know what I am trying to think of? I am trying to think of the name of Axel Munthe's book—the title. I saw the book in my mother's room every day for nearly eighteen years of my life and I can remember everything in her room, Lily. I can remember the pictures on the wall—a picture of Venice with a gondolier in it. I remember her chaise longue with the folded paisley blanket, and next to the chaise longue, on a wobbly little table, my mother, I remember, kept her sewing basket with these little silver scissors I liked. The scissors were in the shape of a bird, a crane sort of—the scissor part was his beak—and when I was little I was always badgering my mother to let me use these scissors and my mother was always saying no to me. The scissors, she said, were too sharp, until finally, one day while my mother was out, I cut myself."

I said, "Molly, I know what you mean. I did the same thing

58

while I was looking for my ring. I had to have a tetanus shot. It was at night. Who knows what I cut myself on. The streets are full of garbage, Molly."

Molly said, "Garbage? What? I can hardly hear you, Lily."

I said, "Hello—Molly, I'm going to pick up the phone in the bedroom again."

Molly said, "I agree, Lily—Lily, are you there?"

I said, "Hmm, yes, it's still pouring outside, Molly."

Molly said, "You're right, the streets are a disgrace. When it rains it's even worse—this is what I keep saying to Claude-Marie and to Fred. I keep saying I cannot believe how much garbage there is in the street—garbage even here in Old Saybrook. Bags of—oh, and I just thought of this, Lily—thought of Price dropping his glass in the street. The time I first met Inez, the time I was telling you about when Inez was sunbathing nude, and Price came up on the roof and he started to tell us a story about the only person, as far as he knew, who had fallen off the Eiffel Tower—a workman. Price said he had read this in a book, and all the workmen had to go up on foot because the elevator was not installed until the Eiffel Tower was completed, and I remember I asked Price: What about lunch? Did the workmen have to come down on foot for lunch? I said: You know how the French are about lunch. I don't remember what Price answered, but I do remember Price was drinking a gin-and-tonic—I told you how it was so hot up there, a hundred degrees in the shade, at least—and Inez had put on her blue-and-white kimono, and Inez said something to Price about how she wished she had gone to Paris too, so she could join in the conversation, and I told Inez that I had never been up the Eiffel Tower either. But Bibi had, I said. Bibi went up the Eiffel Tower with her school. Afterwards, Bibi said how she could see Mademoiselle Boudemange's apartment from the top and from where she was standing. But what Price said then was that it was too hot there for him on the roof. He couldn't take it, Price said. Right after this, Price, who is so tall—Price, you know, is much taller than Claude-Marie—must have hit his head as he was climbing back down the fire escape. Inez and I heard the crack. We heard Price say: Shit. Price must have dropped his glass of gin-and-tonic in the street. Luckily, Price did not kill anybody. It always amazes me, Lily, how more things don't fall down in the street—flower pots, cornices, bits of buildings."

I said, "The very thing I was about to say—Mrs. Davidson, Molly. Mrs. Davidson was my mother's best friend. She jumped out the window and went right through the awning of her apartment building. I was only a little girl but I remember the jagged hole in the canvas before they got around to replacing the awning, and I also remember my mother saying: I pray to God Estelle Davidson died before she hit the cement."

Molly said, "I know. I try not to think about things like this either—things like Patricia, Lily, things like the cat—oh, the cat, Lily, did not die right away either. I only broke his back. The cat went kind of looping head over tail in the driveway. Blood was gushing out of his ears, Lily, gushing out of his mouth. I had to run him over again. The second time was even worse. I was not in reverse. I was going against my instincts. The other thing—I thought of this at the time—was what if someone had seen me? A neighbor. That person, Lily, would have thought I was running over Alicia Thomas's cat on purpose. The Thomases had just moved in, they had bought Suzanne and Harry's old house. Mr. Thomas worked at the Mystic Seaport and the Thomases were black, and I did not go to the cocktail party. The cocktail party Fred gave to welcome them to the neighborhood, and Fred, Lily, went to a lot of trouble. Fred rented a tent in case the weather changed and it started to rain, and Havier said he drank Tab all night, and Claude-Marie had a good time, he said. Claude-Marie said he met a woman who said she loved his accent and who was ready now, she said, to start collecting modern art."

I said, "The cat reminds me of Jason—poor Jason. I hate to talk about Jason, Molly."

Molly said, "Claude-Marie likes people. Claude-Marie likes parties. So did Inez. Remember the birthday party, Lily? Remember what's-his-name, the playwright who lived in Inez's building who dressed up as the gorilla? Inez use to play mah-jong with him, which makes me wonder all of a sudden—wonder about the mah-jong set. Claude-Marie did not mention mah-jong. No one mentioned mah-jong. The mah-jong set, I know, came from Hong Kong. The tiles were real ivory, Lily—not plastic."

I said, "Hong Kong—oh, I want to go to Hong Kong, Molly."

Molly said, "No, the playwright is from Ceylon or from Sri Lanka, and his girlfriend, now I remember, plays with the Philharmonic Orchestra. She is the one, Lily, whom I was telling you about who was stuck in the elevator the time I could hear her shouting. She must be accident prone—not only did she get stuck in the elevator, she was also standing down in the street when Price dropped his glass of gin-and-tonic and the glass nearly hit her. Oh—but the elevator, Lily, is another reason why I prefer to live in a house. A house like the house on the rue Madame. Also, it is in a good neighborhood. After school and in the afternoon when she was little, Bibi could cross the street and play in the Luxembourg. The Luxembourg Garden is a real blessing was what I used to tell her—there is a toy boat basin, a marionette theater, there are ponies and donkeys for hire, although as I told Bibi: You also have to be careful—not just careful of the ponies and donkeys—careful of the pickpockets and the exhibitionists. In Paris, Lily, there are exhibitionists everywhere—it's not just me, Lily, and you know how some people attract them? One time—did I tell you this—it was right after I had arrived in Paris and it was right after I had met Matisse in the south of France, and I went to the theater by myself, Lily—and guess what happened? The man sitting next to me unzipped his pants and stuck his hat over his thing. The play—I'll never forget—was a play by Paul Claudel—something about a satin slipper. A play in five acts that lasted over four hours with one intermission and the whole time, Lily, I was trying to think of the word for penis. I did not speak French yet. I only knew words like: What is the cost of my aunt's pencil?"

I said, "*Combien coute le crayon de ma tante?* You see, I still remember some of my French—oh, but this reminds me, Molly—Patricia. What happened to Patricia in Italy?"

Molly said, "Oh, Lily, Lily, I wish I could describe this to you the way Inez described this to me: How they had to shoot the horse, how Patricia fainted and they had a hard time reviving her, how this, Inez said, despite the hundreds of hours of analysis and the electroshock treatments was like a real death experience for her, and did I know what she, Inez, was talking about? I said: Inez, of course, you are talking about those near-death experiences when people are pronounced clinically dead, then after they are brought back to life again, they tell everyone how they left their bodies and saw a bright yellow light. The same kind of near-death experiences the soldiers who were in Vietnam talk about. Only mostly, the soldiers don't want to or cannot talk about this, and I told Inez—yes, the same thing happened to me when I went skiing."

I said, "Skiing? Molly, I didn't know you knew how to ski. You didn't tell me you knew how to ski."

Molly said, "The French-Canadian journalist told me skiing was easy. He said, in no time at all, I would learn."

I said, "Who? Molly, it's late. It's almost three-thirty."

Molly said, "The French-Canadian journalist who introduced me to Matisse, Lily. The French-Canadian journalist also broke his leg in two places, which brings me back to what I was saying. I was saying how I had never seen snow before except for maybe one or two freak snowstorms in Virginia, and most of the time in that ski resort in Austria, I took lessons— except for this one day. This one day, I guess, I was sick of the lessons and this one day I went to the top of the mountain by myself or maybe—I am not sure about this, Lily—I went to the top of the mountain with the French-Canadian journalist. The French-Canadian journalist was an expert skier— he learned how to ski, he said, at the same time that he learned how to walk, and he skied down the mountain some other way, on a more challenging and difficult run, I guess, while I—I started down the mountain alone. I had no idea. The snow that day was icy and I must have gotten frightened. Right away and near the top of the mountain, Lily, my skis crossed and I fell. I started to slide. I could not stop myself. Instead, I kept sliding down the mountain faster and faster. There was nothing there, Lily, to slow me down or to stop me. There was nothing there to dig my skis or my poles into. Then one of my skis came off. The ski was hanging by the safety strap and the ski kept twisting around and hitting me. But the worst part was the mountain. The whole mountain, Lily, I swear to you, was a sheet of ice and below me in the valley, I could see the village of San Anton. I could see the hotel where we were staying—me and the French-Canadian journalist. The windows of the hotel, I remember, were wide open and the eiderdowns were airing on the window sills. It was amazing, Lily. I could see everything so clearly. I could see the stores, the sports store where I had rented my skis and my equipment. The café, too. I could see the café where, each evening before dinner, the French-Canadian journalist and I would drink hot spicy red wine with cinnamon and cloves in it—but mainly what I focused on was the gas station. The gas station at the entrance of the village of San Anton, and I remember how I watched a car drive into the gas station—a red BMW—and I was watching how the gas attendant was unscrewing the gas cap from the fender of the red BMW and how he was putting in the hose and then, how he was walking around to the front of the car and how he was lifting up the hood of the red BMW and all the time, Lily, I was sliding faster and faster down the mountain and I was sure I was going to be killed, I was sure I was going to die. The funny part was that even while I knew absolutely, Lily, that I was going to die, at the same time, I was also thinking: How stupid this is. Here I am and all I am doing is looking at this gas station and at the gas station at- tendant and at this red BMW car and I should really be seeing something wonderful, something worthwhile. Something, you know, like a vision or a tableau. A tableau of the apostles, for instance, and even if I am not religious, a tableau of maybe Jesus. Jesus bearing his cross with the lovely sad expression on his face. If not this, then why, I asked myself, why weren't the significant events of my life flashing by in front of my eyes the way they are supposed to? Like snapshots. Like the snap- shots of my Charlottesville high school graduation. The pho- tograph where we are all lined up according to size and where the girls are all wearing hats. Or the photograph my father took of me the time I won the English composition prize for a story I called 'Mayhem.' Or a nice snapshot of the first boy

I ever fell in love with—no, not Charlie. And why was it, I kept asking myself, why was it that I was just looking down at the village of San Anton and at the dumb garage and at the man pumping gas and checking the oil of a car? It was so boring, so mundane, so banal. In the end too, of course, I managed to stop myself. The amazing thing is that I did not break anything. I was just bruised. Bruised in funny places, Lily. Under my arms and where the loose ski had hit me probably. The other thing, Lily, when I pulled myself together enough to ski the rest of the way down the mountain, was that the man in the garage still had his head inside the hood of the car, and I swear to you, Lily, I felt as if I had X-ray vision. I could see the dipstick. I could see the oil on it."

I said, "I guess I've been lucky. I've never broken anything skiing. I've twisted things. I sprained my knee once. I wear a bandage for support, a knee brace when I ski."

Molly said, "The French-Canadian journalist had to go back in an ambulance. I never saw him again. I wrote to him in the hospital and he sent me a copy of the interview. The newspaper too, sent me a check for the picture I took. I know I have it here. Lily, I mean the interview. When I find it, I'll read it to you. I cashed the check. I spent the money on the Leica—the Leica I sold to Yuri. The old Leica. The Leica without a built-in light meter. I told Yuri it had a better lens."

I said, "Molly, yes—but Patricia?"

Molly said, "Patricia? Oh, yes, Inez. When I told Inez about my near-death experience skiing, Inez said: Oh, my, but this is a coincidence!"

I said, "Inez did not know how to ski, Molly. Inez did not know how to swim either, and it's three-thirty in the morning now, exactly, Molly. I told you how my watch is ten minutes fast."

Molly said, "I meant how the French-Canadian journalist broke his leg, and Inez said how this was like her father having the heart attack—the heart attack in the other woman's arms—and remember, Lily, how Inez said she was away on the school camping trip? Inez said how it was after she and the kids in her eighth-grade class had hiked up all day to this lake and they were in bed in their sleeping bags, and Inez said how it was strange and no one was used to sleeping on the ground outside looking up at the stars. Everyone, Inez said, kept whispering. The teacher who had come with them had to keep telling them to pipe down and be quiet and finally, Inez said, everyone was. Everyone, Inez said, she guessed was tired from hiking to the lake and anyway, it must have been sometime later and she must have been asleep for a couple of hours because when she woke up, she noticed, Inez said, that none of the stars, the Big Dipper, the Little Dipper—the stars she was familiar with, the stars she had been looking at—were there. There was a whole set of new stars in the sky, and Inez also said how, at first, she just heard regular breathing, then she heard another noise, a noise she was not familiar with either. The noise, she said, she guessed was what woke her up. The noise, she said, frightened her, too. Inez said she thought of moose and of bear. She also thought of calling out to the teacher—the teacher whose name was Miss Hilary. Inez told me she would never forget her name—Miss Hilary. Miss Hilary, she said, was the math teacher. But eventually, Inez said, her eyes got accustomed to the dark and she figured out where the noise was coming from and what it was. Of course, Miss Hilary did not die. Miss Hilary and the kid did not have heart attacks either, only it was a sign. Inez said it was like if you see someone in the street and if, for a minute, you think that person is someone else—someone perhaps that you do not ordinarily think of—and even if you right away realize your mistake, chances are, Inez said, you are likely to run into this very person—the person the first person you saw made me think of—and this kind of thing, Inez said, happened to her a lot. The same thing was true of a word, a phrase, she said. Say, a word like *palimpsest* or a word like *innumerate* that you had never heard of before and that you didn't even know what the word meant and all of a sudden you heard the same word all the time and all over the place. Everyone used it, and this was what Inez said she meant about Miss Hilary and the eighth grade kid in the sleeping bag. Inez said she had never heard anyone making love before and this was the coincidence she was talking about."

I said, "I know what innumerate means. It means someone who does not know anything about numbers. What does palimpsest mean?"

Molly said, "Wait—something to do with stone carvings. Too bad, the French count would have known. Archaeology was his hobby and the French count spoke beautiful English. The French count liked to poke around old castles, old churches—oh, the French count was also a devout Catholic. As a matter of fact, you won't believe this, Lily, the day I met him, a Sunday, the count stopped the car—the Lancia—first, he had to go to Mass he said, and how can I explain this? Kneeling next to him in church felt more intimate than going to bed with him."

I said, "Jim and I used to meditate. We sat on the floor cross-legged, but I could never really concentrate—concentrate on nothing. The whole time I would think of things like: Has Jim taken out the garbage yet? Why hasn't Jim fixed the window? The window that sticks. Oh—he never did, Molly. I still can't open the window."

Molly said, "Who was it? Was it Kevin? It was Kevin, Inez said, who tried to clear himself of traumatic childhood experiences by holding a soup can—Kevin is one of those scientologists, Lily. Kevin also told Inez that ideally you are supposed to go all the way back to the birth canal, but Kevin said he only got as far back as his circumcision. Malcolm, Price's art teacher—at the out-of-body Institute he is always talking about—said he regressed much further. Malcolm said thank the Lord he was not circumcized and thank the Lord he got all the way back to Atlantis—you should have heard him. Each time Malcolm talks about Atlantis, he trots out his other moon theory for you—oh, I should call Malcolm in East Hampton—and the kimono, Lily. I should call Claude-Marie in the morning—the blue-and-white kimono and the gardenias."

I said, "The kimono—I told you, didn't I, Molly, how I spilled *sake* on it? To make matters worse, Jim's boss smoked and he burned a hole in it. You should have seen me, Molly. I was frantic. I told the dry-cleaner: Do the best you can, I don't care what it costs me—oh, speaking of money, Molly, this phone call is costing you a small fortune, it is almost four o'clock in the morning. It is twenty to four in the morning."

Molly said, "And can you believe it—I am still sitting here at my desk sorting through things—sorting through bills? But Claude-Marie pays for the utilities. The phone bill and the electricity. Claude-Marie says it is business and long distance is cheaper after midnight. Anyway, I never go to bed before one or two in the morning. Claude-Marie snores, and, Lily, you should hear the cat. The cat purrs. Most nights, I move out. I try to sleep in the living room. The same thing happens when I go to the city and how many nights, I ask you, Lily, have I spent on Inez's couch? I never sleep a wink or shut my eyes—oh, not because of the couch. The couch is perfectly comfortable. The noise outside—the traffic. The noise of the garbage trucks—oh, God. You should hear them—what I keep telling Claude-Marie: I have never seen so much garbage in my life. Bags and bags of garbage—even in front of the church. The church across the street in Old Saybrook, Lily, the Church of the Holy Redeemer, and I have told Claude-Marie: One day, I am going to go in there and ask someone. Yes, I am—just watch me, I said. I am going to ask the minister or the priest. I am going to say: Father, please tell me, what is inside all those bags? Unused prayer books? Uneaten wafers? But you should hear Claude-Marie on the subject. Not only does Claude-Marie accuse me of always exaggerating, Claude-Marie, Lily, accuses me of having a bag-lady mentality. You would be surprised, too, I have told Claude-Marie, at the number of things I have found, not to mention the seagull. The seagull does not count. Oh, the scarf. The scarf does not count either. I lost Inez's scarf. The scarf Inez was knitting Price for Christmas a couple of years ago. Inez was learning how to knit, she said, and Inez also said how knitting should be easy—no different from plucking a chicken which was what Inez said she did as a girl in Wisconsin. What else did Inez say about those poor chickens? Oh, Inez said how she and Patricia used to sit outside in the yard, each with a dead chicken in her lap, and they would race each other and Inez said how she always won. This was, Inez said, before her father died, before they sold the farm—but what was I saying? Oh, yes, Inez kept dropping stitches in her knitting—the scarf, too, Lily, was all lopsided, the scarf was full of knots and I told Inez not to worry, I would get the scarf back to her in plenty of time before Christmas. After all, I said to Inez, this was only Labor Day Weekend.

Labor Day Weekend, I am sure of this, Lily—Price and Inez were on their way up to pick up Matthew at a camp in New Hampshire."

I said, "When I was a girl, Molly, I went to a camp in Maine."

Molly said, "I told Inez I must have left the scarf on the train. I told Inez I did not do this on purpose. I also told Inez the train was late and I was on my way to the hairdresser. I had an appointment for a haircut—me and my washed-out blond hair."

I said, "Molly, I've told you, you have wonderful hair."

Molly said, "I thought Inez would never forgive me. Inez said the scarf itself was not important to her. The scarf, Inez said, was only symbolic. Sometimes Inez, Lily, could be very rigid, and what I said to her was: Inez, are you sure you won't change your mind and take one? Claude-Marie, I told Inez, liked the photocopies of the scarf better than those of the seagull. The photocopies of Inez's scarf, Claude-Marie said, reminded him of Yuri's paintings—the paintings of legless chairs—hello, Lily, are you listening?"

I said, "Yuri? I hardly know Yuri, Molly. I met Yuri at the Vietnamese restaurant—oh, ha, ha, you can't compare Yuri's hair. Yuri's hair is thick and coarse—you could mop a kitchen floor or tie a boat with it."

Molly said, "Lily, you misunderstood me. I was speaking of Inez's scarf, but now since you mention it, Yuri's hair reminds me of what Nora said the time Yuri came to New York for his opening, the time too, Nora said she got fed up —not just fed up with the lobsters—but fed up, Nora said, on her way to the kitchen to fix breakfast, when she had to walk through the living room, past the sofa bed Yuri was sleeping on—the same sofa bed, I told you already, Claude-

Marie is sleeping on right this minute, the same sofa bed Nora's sister, Mercedes, slept on—and each morning, Nora said she could see another and a different head of hair sticking out from the sofa bed covers. A blond head, a brown head, a black head of hair. One morning, Nora said she saw a pink head of hair. The same morning, Yuri was lying stark naked on top of the sofa bed covers, and this was the day Nora said she had enough, she was fed up, the day she yelled at Ivan: *Those fucking Russians.* Luckily, Ivan did not walk out. Luckily too, Ivan is from Tiflis. First, Ivan says, he is a Georgian, then a Russian second. Like me, Lily. I say I am a Virginian. So did my father. My mother too, and my mother, Lily, was not even born in Virginia, Lily. My mother was born in New Orleans."

I said, "Oh, New Orleans? I have some relatives from New Orleans. Maybe we are related, Molly. Wouldn't this be amazing? Wouldn't this be an incredible coincidence?"

Molly said, "My mother's family had a large house on St. Charles Avenue, and although I was little, I will never forget the house, Lily. The house was filled with bullets. Yes, bullets. Everywhere. In every room. My grandfather collected bullets. He had all kinds—bullets from all different countries, bullets from all different wars and guns. One bullet, Lily, I remember especially. The bullet had teeth marks on it. My grandfather used to say how this particular bullet was found near a Civil War field hospital. My grandfather said how the wounded soldiers chewed on this bullet—the soldiers who were being operated on or who were being amputated. You know—bite the bullet, Lily."

I said, "Oh—oh, yes."

Molly said, "I have always wondered whether this was a true story or whether this was just a story my grandfather had made up—whether my grandfather was pulling my leg. Also, my grandfather had this dog, Lily, a Lab."

I said, "Oh, Jason was a Lab, Molly. A golden Labrador retriever."

Molly said, "This dog—I cannot remember his name—was a black Labrador. My grandfather used to go duck hunting with him on Lake Pontchartrain, but what I was going to say about the bullet—"

I said, "Oh, the dog chewed the bullet, Molly—your grandfather made up the whole story, Molly."

Molly said, "You know how children are—I really wanted to have this bullet. I wanted this bullet more than I ever wanted anything else in my whole life, in the whole world. Each time I went to visit my grandfather, I would beg him. I would badger him to give me the bullet. I even thought up ways of stealing the bullet from him, Lily, but then you know what happened? You know what happened to the bullet, Lily? The day my grandfather died, the dog ate the bullet. Yes, the black Lab. The very same day—how about this for a coincidence, Lily?"

I said, "Amazing—but no, Jason had the softest mouth. Jason could pick up an egg in his mouth without cracking the shell. I swear this is true. One time, Jason picked up a whole family of newborn rabbits he had found in the bushes somewhere. Jason brought each baby rabbit one by one over to Sam and me—the rabbits were tiny, Molly, you should have seen their ears—and you know what the only trouble was, Molly? The only trouble was that each of these baby rabbits got drowned to death in Jason's own saliva. Ironic, isn't it? What did you say before? What did you say Claude-Marie always says? No good deed goes unpunished?"

Molly said, "The dog, my grandfather's dog, Lily, the black Lab, was fine. We even got the bullet back. But the funny thing was that now, with my grandfather gone, I no longer wanted this bullet. I had lost interest in the bullet completely—but, speaking of coincidences, Inez, I am sure, would have gotten a kick out of this story."

I said, "Yes, signs were what Inez was always talking about. Inez was going to do my chart. I am a Libra. I was born the same day Natalie Wood was—October eleventh. When is your birthday, Molly?"

Molly said, "Oh, let's not talk about birthdays. I told Inez: It's useless. I don't know what time I was born and the only thing my mother said she can remember is that it must have been at a quarter past something. I was born at home, and the whole time, my mother said, she could hear the grandfather clock in the hallway. The grandfather clock chimed every quarter of an hour and made her crazy. The clock, too, was always slow, Lily. The clock lost several minutes a day, and a man from Switzerland came up all the way from Richmond to try to fix it. I will never forget this either—perhaps you are right and I do attract perverts—the man exposed himself to me, Lily."

I said, "But did he fix the clock, Molly?"

Molly said, "I don't remember. I only remember his thing, which may be the reason why I am chronically late and why Claude-Marie says I have no sense of time—none at all. Claude-Marie may be right. Oh, and how long have we been talking on the phone, Lily? To me, it feels like just a few minutes. Inez had no sense of time either. Inez kept me waiting for half an hour outside the restaurant. I got soaking wet. My shoes, I told you already, Lily. Luckily, I did not catch pneumonia. Pneumonia is the last thing I need now that we have to sell this house in Connecticut, now that I have to pack up everything including the cat, and now that Claude-Marie says he wants to go back to France and I want Bibi to go to camp."

I said, "Camp? Did I tell you, Molly, that I went to a camp

in Maine for three summers in a row? We slept in tents and I learned how to play tennis and how to capsize a canoe and get it right side up again."

Molly said, "Hello? I can't hear you, Lily—Matthew told Inez he hated his camp in New Hampshire. Maybe I should send Bibi out West and to some place like Montana, away from Jerome and away from France."

I said, "Hello? I can't hear you either, Molly. The time Jim and I drove out West, we drove through Utah and Nevada. I thought Utah would never end—those salt flats are endless and, wouldn't you know it, we ran out of gas in the desert. I knew we would. I told Jim if only he would please listen— listen to me. Jim had to hitchhike a ride. He left me alone in the car. The nearest next town was forty miles. I'll never forget this."

Molly said, "I had to hitchhike with Bibi once. The time I took Bibi to see the abandoned razor blade factory. After the count died, Lily, they tore it down. Bibi and I watched while this big steel ball knocked down the walls—mustard-colored cement walls—and you should have seen us, Bibi and I were covered in yellow dust, and on the way home, we took the wrong bus. We ended up lost in the Renault car factory and a workman drove us back in his Peugeot. I am trying to re-member his name, Lily. Isn't this silly? In the car, on the way back to the rue Madame, we had a conversation. The workman said he was not really a Renault factory worker, he said he was an artist, and guess what I said? Blah, blah, blah, you must show Claude-Marie, my husband, your art. Of course, you know what Claude-Marie said to me afterwards, and Claude-Marie also said the paintings were dreadful. The paint-ings were all of smashed cars—oh, Charles. This was another one of these amazing coincidences. The workman's name was Charles, and Charles, of course, was the name of the French count. I told you, didn't I, how the French count was named after his father and the count's father was named after his and so on and so forth? Personally, I have never liked the idea of naming children after their parents. Look at Price Junior, and when Bibi was born, I said to Claude-Marie it would be too confusing. I also said: Look at the Miss Marys, for instance."

I said, "Who? The Miss who?"

Molly said, "The Miss Marys are two eccentric old ladies who lived next door to us in Crozet. They are the same ones Claude-Marie brings up each time Claude-Marie talks about my mother and how all Southerners are crazy anyhow, which reminds me—remember how Yuri kept telling everyone how his mother knew Chekhov? Well, I told Yuri my mother knew Faulkner. William Faulkner. She certainly did, Lily. William Faulkner lived in Charlottesville, so did poor old Anastasia—remember? Anastasia—oh, and I should have told Yuri this—Anastasia was the woman who claimed she was the only surviving daughter of the Czar of Russia. Poor Anastasia. The reporters were always pestering her and asking her questions—questions like what kind of jelly did the Romanovs have each morning for breakfast? And in 1917, how old exactly was the royal family dog?"

I said, "Mrs. Shubatoff, my art teacher in school, Molly, was a White Russian. Mrs. Shubatoff told us how she had escaped from the revolution by giving each person along the way who helped her a button. A pearl button. The buttons on Mrs. Shubatoff's dress were genuine pearls, Molly. I don't know why but this story stays in my head and I used to worry about her. I used to worry that by the time Mrs. Shubatoff reached wherever she said she was finally going, her dress would be flapping wide open."

Molly said, "All kinds of people live in Virginia, and I have said this before to Claude-Marie: Look at Matisse. I said Henri Matisse. I know, I know, Matisse did not live in Virginia but Matisse was no different. Blood is thicker than water, I said."

I said, "I told you, didn't I, Molly, my brother lives in Virginia? My brother William."

Molly said, "Inez, too—blood is thicker than water, I mean —even if Inez did not get along with her sister, Patricia. Patricia is so different. Patricia looks more like Inez's mother —remember? Inez's mother was the one who stood up and made the toast at the surprise birthday party. Inez's mother was the one who said that after this she counted her blessings and that something like this made her realize how fragile life is and how she had to enjoy every minute of it. I agree with her completely, Lily, but Inez's mother was talking about her second husband, Inez's stepfather, the CEO. Inez's mother was talking about how when her second husband was flying back from Hawaii, all of a sudden something in the plane exploded. The passengers sitting right in front of him in Business Class were sucked right out of the plane and into the Pacific Ocean. Inez's stepfather said that there was this hole in the plane and a lot of shoes and briefcases went flying past him and the woman sitting next to him was screaming that she knew one of those people, one of those people, she said, was related to her. Inez's stepfather also said how he had told the reporters that one minute those passengers were ordering drinks from the stewardess and that the next minute they were gone. And everything Inez's stepfather said he told the reporters was later misquoted in the paper. Inez's stepfather said he remembered for instance, exactly what kind of drinks those passengers who had been sucked out of the plane had ordered. One woman, he said, had ordered a Bloody Mary and the man sitting next to her had asked for a double Scotch and water. Inez's stepfather said he could swear to this even if this had occurred early in the morning. The point of the story, he said, was how unreliable reporters were. All writers, I told Inez's stepfather at the party, are unreliable. They are also opportunistic, I said."

I said, "Inez's stepfather should meet Michelle, Molly. Remember the book she wrote? Her supposed autobiography? But it's hard to believe that the birthday party was so long ago already. Who else was there? Mercedes was there, remember? Mercedes was wearing that low-cut black dress. So was Roberta. I mean Roberta was there. I always forget about Roberta."

Molly said, "Poor Roberta. And poor Inez—oh, yes, Mercedes's dress. How can I ever forget that dress? You are right, Lily, women have instincts. Women have a sixth sense about these things, the way men never have, and I have told Claude-Marie, Lily, if it had not been for the busybody in the grocery store, Claude-Marie would never have known. The same thing goes for Price, Lily. If the bus had not broken down and Price had not hitchhiked back to the village instead of hitchhiking on to Toledo to buy his paint brushes, he would never have found out about Jesus what's-his-name."

I said, "Ramirez, Molly. Oh, I don't know what made me think of this now—the story Inez told me—no, not about Jesus Ramirez, about the woman, the woman—oh, now it is all coming back to me. The king of Portugal wanted to marry—no, no, Molly, this is not a joke, this is not the king of Sweden—"

Molly said, "Norway—I told you, I can never remember jokes either, it must be Ivan's accent. Ivan is also a good mimic. Have you ever heard him? You would die laughing, Lily. The way Ivan can imitate Yuri, the way Ivan said Yuri brought along a bottle of vodka on the bus—the kind of vodka with a blade of grass floating in it—and by the time the bus pulled up in front of the casino in Atlantic City, Yuri was singing something out of *Boris Gudonov*, he was singing at the top of his lungs. It makes me laugh just to think about this, and you know how all those people are always marching in the opera. Marching to Moscow or, who knows, marching from Moscow —oh, here, I found a letter from Dominique."

I said, "Molly—can you let me finish?"

Molly said, "Oh—go ahead, Lily. I'm listening. Dominique says here that she has gotten her real estate license and that she hope to sell this big house and with the money she makes she will blah, blah, blah."

I said, "Molly—I just want to tell you what Inez said."

Molly said, "I am, Lily. I am listening. Oh, Dominique says with the money she makes she is going to buy a new car. A Peugeot. There, I'm throwing her letter in the garbage, Lily."

I said, "I throw everything away. I never save anything. Yes, but what was I saying? Oh, the story Inez told me. A story about how the king of Portugal was in love with a woman named Inez—yes, her name was also Inez—only the king's ministers were against the match and instead of letting the king marry Inez, they murdered her—they murdered Inez de Castro—and the king—I have forgotten his name—to show the ministers that he would always love Inez anyway, unearthed the corpse and sat the corpse of Inez on the throne next to him. The king made the court pay homage to the dead queen, to Inez de Castro. Can you imagine, Molly—imagine the corpse rotting away there on the throne? Can you imagine the smell? Molly—is this apocryphal or what? Molly—are you listening to me?"

Molly said, "Yes. What time is it, now?"

I said, "Four—yes, four in the morning, Molly."

Molly said, "Hmmm."

I said, "I'm just thinking—thinking about Inez."

Molly said, "Hmmm. Yes. Poor Inez."

I said, "Yes, I mean the real Inez—not the story. The story is just a legend, Molly."

Molly said, "Hmm—hard to imagine, isn't it? Inez what's-her-name sitting decomposing on the throne."

I said, "De Castro. I mean the real Inez."

Molly said, "Yes, poor Inez in her underwear and boots—the galoshes."

I said, "Oh, the galoshes. I almost forgot about the galoshes, Molly, and I wish it would stop raining soon."

Molly said, "I know, it's been raining for days and I wonder—should I call Roberta now? I hate it when the phone rings in the middle of the night. It's always bad news or the wrong number."

I said, "Poor Roberta."

Molly said, "Have you seen Roberta since she dyed her hair that awful red? I told Roberta it was the same red as the sweater Claude-Marie gave me, the red that turns purple, and the red that French women like Madame Florisson's daughter-in-law dye their hair. Madame Florisson's daughter-in-law, Lily, is the one with the kidney disease about whom Claude-Marie said the dialysis machine came in the nick of time or it would have been the ball game for her, only Claude-Marie said this to me in French—*la fin du match*. I told you how Claude-Marie loves going to football games, but in France it is soccer, and I stay at home or else I go for a walk with Bibi. I take Bibi out for an ice-cream cone, except Bibi has started to count calories. Jerome or someone must have said something. But

Bibi is thin, Lily. Bibi is skinny. What is that old saying—
something about how one is never quite rich or quite thin
enough? Inez, too, come to think of it. The last time I saw
Inez at the restaurant, Inez said she was going on a diet—a
pasta diet. Inez ordered pasta with a cream seafood sauce,
and Inez said she only ordered the sauce out of curiosity. I
ordered a salad. A *salade Niçoise*—you know, tuna fish, to-
matoes, olives—and each time I eat this salad, Lily, I always
think of Matisse and of the south of France. This salad and a
carafe of red wine was exactly what the French-Canadian journalist and I ordered for lunch the day he interviewed Matisse
and the day I took the picture. The restaurant, Lily, was in
the same village Matisse lived in, and I'll never forget this
either, Lily, how when we were finished and the French-
Canadian journalist asked for the bill and for directions—
directions to Matisse's house—the owner of the restaurant said
oh, if only he had known, he would never have charged us a
thing for the meal."

I said, "I told you about the time in Mexico when I ate the
iguana and we didn't pay for that either, except you should
have seen me, Molly—I was about ready to go to the hospital."

Molly said, "Claude-Marie, on account of the war—oh,
Lily, I can't even talk about this—Claude-Marie also said he
did not know the difference. Claude-Marie said he thought it
was a rabbit. Can you imagine? Oh, and when Bibi heard
about this, Lily—poor Bibi—Bibi nearly got sick to her stomach. You know how sensitive children are—but what was I
saying? Oh, how Inez said she wanted to lose weight, how
Inez said she was on a diet now, and I said to Inez: Inez, look
at me. I have not gained an ounce. I wear the same size since
before I got married and since before I got pregnant. It's true,
Lily, I probably still own the pair of jeans I wore when I met
Matisse. And women did not wear jeans then. I remember

that Matisse made a remark about them. You would be surprised, Lily—Matisse was still pretty sharp then. He still had an eye. But I wear blue jeans everywhere now. I wear them to restaurants, I wear them to openings, and the only place to buy good jeans in France, Lily, is at Bon Marché. Bon Marché, Lily, is the only store in Paris that has jeans that fit me, and Bon Marché is right around the corner from Mademoiselle Boudemange's apartment where Bibi goes for her piano lessons. Bibi's piano lesson lasts about an hour and this gives me time to do my shopping or else I go and sit in a café and have a cup of coffee. The same café—oh, yes, they know me there. I don't remember the name of it, the café that is right off rue Madame on the corner of rue Nôtre-Dame-des-Champs and rue Vavin."

I said, "Oh, something I have always been meaning to ask you—what does rue Madame stand for, Molly? Madame who?"

Molly said, "Funny you should ask, Lily. I've often asked myself the same thing. There is a rue Monsieur le Prince and no one knows who Monsieur le Prince was, either. But you would think after all these years—how long have I been living in France, Lily? I hate to think—time goes by much too quickly—I can remember the first time I sailed to France on the *Queen Mary* as if it were yesterday. I also remember how I had to promise my mother that I would be back in time for Miss Mary's summer solstice recital—the artistic Miss Mary, not the Miss Mary who cleaned the house and planted the vegetable garden. You should have heard her, Lily. Miss Mary always read the same poems by Dante Gabriel Rossetti and by Christina Georgina, his sister."

I said, "Oh, God, don't tell me. But were you back in time for the recital, Molly?"

Molly said, "Oh, this was such a long time ago, Lily, I no

longer remember. But I do remember how those two Miss
Marys lived together and how, after school, my friend Amy
and I used to visit them. We would have to listen to the artistic
Miss Mary tell us how when she used to live in New York—
Miss Mary said she had been an actress or a dancer, I forget
which—she knew all these people like Hume Cronyn and
Jessica Tandy. Ruth Draper, too, was someone else Miss Mary
said she knew intimately. Sometimes Miss Mary would even
do an imitation of a Ruth Draper monologue. I'll never forget
this, Lily, the monologue was called 'The Italian Lesson.' 'The
Italian Lesson' is about a woman who is constantly being
interrupted—the phone rings, her children burst in on her,
the cook, too, interrupts with questions about how many people will there be for dinner, etcetera—so that by the end of
the lesson, the woman has never gotten past *Nel mezzo del
cammin di nostra vita*."

I said, "Oh, 'In the middle of the—' "

Molly said, "I know, and this reminds me of Bibi's piano
lessons. For two years now, Bibi has played nothing but 'Für
Elise.' *Da da da da da da dum*, which almost drives me crazy
but what was I telling you? Oh, about the Miss Marys? What
I remember best was how every year around Christmastime,
the other Miss Mary, the one who planted the garden, the
one who was not artistic, Lily, and the one who did not wear
lipstick, gave me and Amy each a jar of her home put-up
peaches. Miss Mary told us—me and Amy—to be sure to give
the peaches to our parents, and each year, you know what we
did, Lily? Each year, on our way home, we—Amy and I—
threw Miss Mary's jar of peaches into the bushes. Now, in
retrospect and in light of what happened to the Miss Marys,
I feel guilty, to say nothing of the waste. Half a dozen jars of
peaches—and if someone found all those jars lying in the

bushes, what would they think, Lily? The other troubling thing
was when I mentioned this to Amy—although Amy said she
remembered the Miss Marys perfectly—Amy said she did not
remember a thing about the jars of peaches. Amy said what
she remembered best was the time I threw my hat in the
Rivanna River. Amy could even remember the name of the
boy who found it for me, Lily. The boy's name, Amy said,
was Gordon, and Gordon, Amy also said, had something
wrong with his lips. Gordon, she said, talked something like
this: *Nyere's nyour nyat, Nyolly. Nyi nyound nyit nyoating
nyin nye nyiver.* Amy did a perfect imitation of him, Lily,
while I told Amy, I had no memory of this Gordon person—
no, none at all—even though, Amy said, Gordon was in our
class at school. Each year, too, Amy said, Gordon won the
math and comportment prize, except for the one year Gordon's
mother ran away with the Trailways Bus driver and that year,
too, Amy also said, everyone in Crozet talked about nothing
else but Gordon's mother's love-life. Funny, the things you
remember. But chances are I'll never go back to Crozet again."

I said, "My brother, I told you, Molly, is an orthopedic
surgeon and he lives in Richmond. Each year, I go visit William for Thanksgiving, but this year I didn't. This Thanksgiving, William and his wife, Lucille, went to China. William
said he visited hospitals in China. He said he saw all kinds
of surgery being performed without any anesthetic—with
only acupuncture—eye operations, appendectomies—oh, you
won't believe this, Molly—I didn't. I told William: I am no
doctor but this is impossible."

Molly said, "Did you say Richmond? Your brother lives in
Richmond, Lily? I haven't been to Richmond in years—not
since my father died. Richmond was where I used to do my
shopping, Lily, and the last time I went to Richmond was with

Amy to pick up my father's cremains—oh, this is a horrible story, Lily. I will never live this story down, and swear to God, too, this is true and partly Amy's fault. Amy said since we were in Richmond already, we might as well kill two birds with one stone and go to Miller and Rhoads, the department store. Amy bought herself an evening dress. A layered black chiffon with tiny spaghetti straps and no back to it whatsoever. To this day, Lily, I can still see this dress as clear as day, and I remember, I said to Amy: Amy, where on earth are you going to wear a dress like this? To the Farmington Hunt Club Ball?"

I said, "Molly, I have a dress like this, only my dress is not black. My dress is dark blue with little star-shaped gold flecks in it. I bought the dress in Italy the time I went to Marrakesh with Sam and Felicia. The time I told you about when we drove to the Atlas Mountains and Felicia took those pictures out of the car window and the man threw a rock right through the windshield."

Molly said, "Oh, yes, Marrakesh. What is the name of the hotel in Marrakesh? Nora went there for her vacation. Nora said she spent three days in bed with terrible cramps while Mercedes, her sister, got to go everywhere."

I said, "I still wear the dress, Molly. The blue dress with the gold flecks. Come to think of it, I wore the dress the day I met Leonard."

Molly said, "I told Nora I got my period when I was twelve. I was visiting relatives. My relatives in New Orleans, and I told Nora I did not know what to expect. At least Bibi knew. Bibi knows everything. Bibi learned everything from the baby-sitter and, as far as I know and even if she is only nearly fourteen years old, Lily, Bibi could be in bed with Jerome right this minute."

I said, "Isn't there a six-hour time difference? This makes it mid-morning in France. It's the other way around if you are like Leonard and always going to Japan and crossing the international date line. Then it's tomorrow. It's the twenty-fifth already."

Molly said, "Oh, May twenty-fifth is also my dentist appointment, Lily. I told you, Fred is going to drive me, and Fred said he had to go to New London anyway in his pick-up truck to buy flooring for the kitchen. Fred is remodelling, he is doing the whole house himself, Lily—he and Havier—and I told Fred: Fred, you should see our house on rue Madame. The house was built in the eighteenth century. The house is a landmark building. Gertrude Stein and Alice B. Toklas, I told Fred, used to live right around the corner from us on rue de Fleurus, right next to the butcher Claude-Marie always goes to. The same butcher, Lily, who cut off his finger."

I said, "Molly, the time I cut my finger, the cut was so deep, you know what the doctor said to me? He said: Be thankful you are not a concert pianist."

Molly said, "Hello—what did you say, Lily? The butcher cut off his finger right after Claude-Marie had turned the corner of rue de Fleurus with the three veal cutlets he said he had bought for our dinner—a cutlet for each of us, including a little cutlet for Bibi. Veal, I told you, is the only meat Bibi will eat now—and Claude-Marie said how he had had no idea. Claude-Marie said only afterwards, when he caught a glimpse of the ambulance from the living room windows. From the living room windows, Lily, we can also look straight across into our neighbor's apartment, which is why I always try to keep the curtains shut."

I said, "Molly, this reminds me of—who was it? Oh, Inez. Of course, it was Inez who could see out her window—did she tell you this? She told me. Inez told me how she could see right into the bedroom window of the couple who lived opposite her, and like clockwork, Inez said, the couple always made love every Sunday at nine o'clock in the morning. Inez also said how it always took the same exact amount of time for the couple to reach an orgasm—the woman first, the man four minutes afterwards. Oh—and, Molly, this, too. Inez said how sometimes she ran into this same couple in the street or in the deli around the corner from where they both lived, and whenever Inez said she did, Inez said she always automatically looked down at her watch. She could not help it, Inez said, like one of those Pavlovian responses."

Molly said, "Oh—I haven't thought of this in years—I told you how Charlie Gibson was pre-med. Charlie Gibson wanted to become a vet and he had to conduct all these weird experiments—and what was it Charlie Gibson talked about all the time? Oh, anthropomorphism."

I said, "Anthropo—what? Molly, you have to speak into the receiver. I can't hear you."

Molly said, "I said—to Charlie Gibson animals were just like human beings."

I said, "Molly, I know, you should have seen Jason. Jason was like a child to me."

Molly said, "Charlie Gibson, too, owned about a dozen dogs, Lily—little dogs, big dogs, coon dogs, rabbit-hunting dogs, all kinds of dogs. As a matter of fact, Charlie Gibson almost killed me once because of two dogs, Lily. Have I told you this story? You may want to laugh, but it was not funny at the time—no, not a bit. The two dogs were stuck doing you-know-what to each other right on the road to Monticello, on the way up to Thomas Jefferson's house—those two darn dogs, Lily, could have been the death of us. Charlie Gibson was driving, and Charlie Gibson tried to avoid the two dogs, and the car went off the road and turned over. A brand-new car, too, Lily. A sports car that did not belong to Charlie Gibson. A car he had borrowed without asking from the Foreign Sports Motors Car Garage where he worked part-time as a mechanic. Poor Charlie Gibson, he nearly lost his job over that one. Charlie Gibson, Lily, was the type of person who was always in trouble. The Edgar Allan Poe episode was nothing by comparison, and no wonder, I say, Charlie Gibson is in jail now for embezzling pension funds."

I said, "But, Molly, were you all right?"

Molly said, "Not a scratch. Like a miracle was what I said to Charlie Gibson. The dogs, too, Lily. We managed to avoid them. But the car, Lily. The car was demolished. Charlie Gibson had to telephone the garage for a tow truck and his boss, when he answered the phone, did not know what Charlie Gibson was talking about. A tow truck for what? was what Charlie Gibson's boss shouted—I can hear him to this day, Lily. I could hear him then, he was yelling so loud. I'll never forget it, he sounded apoplectic. When Charlie Gibson tried to explain, his boss would not let him. His boss kept right on shouting—shouting: Call the fucking S.P.C.A. then."

I said, "I know men like this—men who shout, Molly. You should have heard Sam, Molly. His voice, I swear, could shatter glass. I remember one time we were at the theater and Sam did not return to his seat in time after the intermission —I don't know where he was—in the bathroom or, more likely, getting a drink or outside smoking a cigarette. The curtain went up and Sam just stood there in the middle of the aisle shouting: Lily! Some people went: Ssh. Others laughed. I was so mortified I could have killed him."

Molly said, "I know what you mean—people are so inconsiderate. Oh—here are a whole bunch of letters from Bibi when she was little."

I said, "Speaking of shouting, you should have heard Kevin. This was in the middle of the day, Molly, Kevin was still in bed in the bedroom. Kevin was shouting at us—at me and Inez and at her friend the playwright from downstairs and from Sri Lanka—that if we didn't stop the damn clack-clacking right this minute, he, Kevin was going to throw the mah-jong set out the window. The mah-jong set was real ivory, Molly, the mah-jong set was expensive, and what I told Inez then was: If ever I get to Hong Kong, I am going to buy myself one just like it."

Molly said, "These letters from Bibi, Lily—I am rereading them and I can't decide whether I should keep them."

I said, "You know me, Molly, I throw everything out. I never save anything. My apartment is too small, there is no room, and this too, was one of the things I kept saying to Inez: Inez, you are so lucky, I said. Inez, you have plenty of room. Inez, you have plenty of space. The only problem, as far as I am concerned, is the location."

Molly said, "Don't forget—the elevator. The elevator, Lily, was a problem."

I said, "If I took a taxi to Inez's house, the taxi, Molly, would end up costing me over ten dollars. Ten dollars is a lot of money was what I used to say to Inez, and this does not include the tip. The tip was extra, Molly."

Molly said, "That's right, that's what I said, and remember I told you Inez could have taken the subway. Yuri did, Lily. Yuri took the subway to Fifty-second Street and I told Yuri to walk the two blocks to the restaurant—to the Italian restaurant, the same restaurant I had lunch at with Inez—and, oh, my God, Lily, you should have seen how much Yuri ate. I have never seen anyone eat as much as Yuri in my whole life. Thank God, too, was what I said to him—thank God, I am not paying for this lunch. Don't forget, Lily, Yuri still owes me two hundred and fifty dollars for my Leica. Hello, hello? Lily, can you hear me?"

I said, "Yes, hello, I can hear you—I was just thinking— Sam had a huge appetite. Sam said he always wanted to try everything at least once, which was why we ate the iguana, Molly."

Molly said, "I am still looking, Lily, looking for the interview and the picture I took. I told you, I was just wearing jeans and a T-shirt and Matisse was wearing a long sleeved white shirt and gray checked hound's tooth cotton slacks. And Matisse, I also remember, was wearing a sweater. *On ne sait jamais*— one never knows—it can turn cold was what Matisse said to me, and Matisse was right, Lily—it did. That night the thermometer dropped thirty degrees."

I said, "With all this rain, it's chilly here, too, Molly. I'm glad I made myself a cup of cocoa—I have terrible circulation, Molly. My hands and feet get freezing cold. The other day— I don't remember why now—I said to Leonard: Cold hands, warm heart, and Leonard told me about how his mother has different kinds of teas—a tea to make her sleep, a tea to keep her awake, a tea so she won't get constipated. Leonard also told me about the special iced tea his mother makes. His mother, Leonard said, makes it with orange juice and I said: Leonard what—orange juice?"

Molly said, "It's funny how you can never find anything when you are looking for it. I know the interview is here somewhere. I told Havier I would find it for him—and speaking of drinking, I tell you, Lily, not drinking has made all the difference to Havier."

I said, "Yes, but I was right, I think, to tell Leonard that Maryland is too hot in the summer. I told Leonard I would visit his mother in September. You've never met Leonard, have you, Molly? Inez did not get to meet Leonard, either. Roberta did. Roberta met Leonard the day she dyed her hair red. I remember, I almost did not recognize her."

Molly said, "Who? Leonard? No. Oh, here's a postcard. A picture postcard from Alicia Thomas I got a few weeks ago—a picture postcard of a bunch of kittens."

I said, "Let me see, I met Leonard right after Victor came back from Nicaragua and right after Victor asked Leslie to marry him. I met Leonard at the party Michelle gave for them. The funny thing was, Molly, Michelle said she used to go out with Leonard, and what Leonard said was he only decided to go to the party at the very last minute and against his better judgment, which was lucky."

Molly said, "Here, Alicia Thomas writes that Marine World cannot compare to Old Saybrook."

I said, "Lucky for me, Molly. I nearly did not go to Michelle's party either. Leslie convinced me. Leslie said it was good for me to go out and meet other people—you've met Leslie, Molly—Leslie is the one who is getting married to Victor, and Leslie is the one to whom I said: Leslie, you are crazy to get tattooed in a place like Managua—what if the needle is not clean? Hello—Molly?"

Molly said, "Charlie Gibson got tattoed while he was in the Navy and while he was drunk. He got a dragon tattooed on his cheek and the cheek I am talking about, Lily, is his other cheek, his you-know-what—ha, ha, ha—and the last time I saw Charlie Gibson, Lily, was the time my father died—oh, I told you the story of how I left the cremains of my father in his white linen suit in a dressing room at Miller and Rhoads, the department store, and how Amy and I only realized that I forgot him when we were halfway back to Charlottesville. We made a U-turn and we drove back to Richmond at one hundred miles an hour, and wouldn't you know it a policeman stopped us for speeding, and when Amy tried to explain to him what had happened, the policeman told Amy that she must be crazy and if ever he caught her again he would revoke her license, but what was I saying? Oh, my father's funeral. You should have seen the church, Lily—the church in Crozet—the church was packed. Everyone was there. The whole Gibson family—they are one of the oldest families in the area—and the Miss Marys. Of course, Amy was there. A whole lot of other people too—people I had completely forgotten about and people I no longer remembered, like the boy with the speech impediment about whom Amy said—I should hear him now, his speech is much improved. What did I say his name was? Gordon?"

I said, "Like Carlos—the simultaneous translator Nora is always talking about. Nora says Carlos only stutters when he is talking and not when he is translating, which, Nora says, has something to do with his concentration. Did I tell you I met Carlos once? Nora had me and Carlos for supper, and you should have heard him, Molly. Carlos asked me to *pa-pa-ppp-pa-ss-ss th-th-e p-pp-pp-pe-pe-pep-pep-pepper pp-pp-pl-ppl-ee-e-ppleea-ss-se.* I didn't know what to do, Molly. I didn't know whether to wait until he had finished or to just go ahead and pass him the pepper anyway. I decided to wait. I thought it was more polite. You never know, do you? With Michelle, too, Molly. I never know whether to mention her book. I only got as far as the middle. I only got as far as when she came to America. I got bogged down when she and her family moved to a town in upstate New York. The only thing

I really remember about Michelle's book, Molly, was about her little brother. Michelle's little brother got sick with diphtheria and they had to bury him at sea. Only you know what, Molly? Michelle made this up. Michelle made up the whole part about her little brother. Michelle admitted this. Michelle admitted it on "Good Morning, America" or on one of those talk shows. I never watch them, do you, Molly? A lot of people do—while they are getting dressed, or while they are eating breakfast. But Michelle said this was not her fault. Michelle said her editor told her to. Amazing really to what lengths people will go—what they will invent for the sake of a good story, for the sake of publicity—invent a little brother. And the other funny thing—Molly, are you there? Are you listening?"

Molly said, "Hmm, yes, I am here. I am listening, Lily. Do you know what time it is? My watch is in the kitchen."

I said, "The funny thing is the made-up part was the part I remember the best—the part that was the most vivid to me, Molly—the part about the brother dying of diphtheria. I remember how Michelle wrote he was so small he could have fit into one of those boxes florists use to put long-stemmed flowers—roses—in. That small. He was only five years old, and Michelle wrote how all the passengers, all of them immigrants like herself and her family, were pressed up together against the ship's railing listening to the captain recite the burial service—'Ashes to ashes, dust to dust'—and although most of the people on board the ship did not understand a word of English, there was not a sound to be heard. Only the sound of the captain's voice and the sound of the waves breaking until her little brother's body slid into the ocean. Then the ship blew its whistle and there was not a single dry eye—including the sailors'—left on board the ship. Me too, Molly, I was crying while I read this. And her little brother's name,

Michelle said, was Lech. Little Lech with blond curly hair who could have fit into a box for long-stemmed roses. Now that I think of this too, Lech isn't even a Jewish name, is it, Molly? So none of this was true. Molly?"

Molly said, "Yes. No. I don't know. I threw away Alicia Thomas's postcard and it must be after four o'clock in the morning, Lily."

I said, "Half past, and Michelle, too, is a lot older than Leonard. How old, I asked Leonard, was Michelle when she first came to America?"

Molly said, "People's relationships never cease to amaze me. People's relationships are a complete mystery to me. Just look at Inez and Kevin, Lily."

I said, "You're right, Molly. Take Leonard. In bed, Leonard is different. You would never know, either, by just talking to him. When I first met Leonard, I did not know what to say to him. I tried everything, Molly. I talked about the ballet, the book I was reading, I even told Leonard about the apartment in Paris with no hot water that we lived in and how I started the pottery lessons."

Molly said, "I know, Lily, time goes by so quickly. I was photocopying Notre Dame then."

I said, "The woman who gave me the pottery lessons, I'll never forget her. Her name was Fiona, and she said she had lived alone in a monastery."

Molly said, "Now I want to photocopy I. M. Pei's pyramid, Lily, only I am sure they won't let me."

I said, "Whose pyramid? Oh, let me think—where was it I read this? I read this recently—an article that said you could live a lot longer if you lived in a pyramid. The article also claimed that if milk was sold in a conical container, the milk, too, would not sour so quickly."

Molly said, "Oh, I must have read the same article, which

also said how inside a pyramid a razor blade would stay sharper, which was why the article caught my eye and made me think: Oh, if only Charles, the French count, was here. Oh, if only Charles could read this article. Funny too, what catches your eye—just look at Inez, for instance. Poor Inez."

I said, "Molly, you are so right, everyone is different, but have I told you already how I used to have the same kind of galoshes—the boots with the buckles? I remember how when I was a child, half the time I could not be bothered to buckle up the buckles. I would walk around with them flapping open and my father would stop me and he would say something to me like: Lily, the one thing I cannot tolerate in a person is carelessness. He would say the same thing to me about being messy or if I was late—whenever he could catch me at something. My father was very critical. I wonder sometimes how my mother put up with him. My mother, Molly, was completely different. My mother—bless her heart—was a free spirit. I told you how she used to go swimming? But what was I saying? Oh, Inez. Yes, Inez."

Molly said, "Poor Inez, and Fiddle made a—oh, I wish I knew what Fiddle stands for—this could drive me crazy, Lily. Probably, Fiddle stands for a name like Lois or Doris, a name I would never think of, which reminds me—don't ask me why—of the day Inez's mother came by and of the day Inez's mother was smoking cigarettes and Inez was opening the window. Inez's mother was talking about this article she had read—an article on plant experiments. Inez's mother told Inez that by piping in different kinds of music to a cornfield in the Midwest, some scientists proved that the corn that had listened to rock-and-roll did not grow as quickly or as tall as the corn that had listened to Mozart."

I said, "When I go to the dentist, Molly, the dentist gives

me a set of earphones. I can choose what kind of music to listen to. He also has books on tape, and the last time I had a filling, I listened to a novel by John Le Carré."

Molly said, "Oh, God, Lily, please don't talk to me about drilling. I have to go to the dentist on Thursday and today is Wednesday already."

I said, "Afterwards, I had to go out and buy the book to see how the story ended, Molly."

Molly said, "The book I am reading now is about a woman in Africa who might or might not have killed her best friend. I thought of lending the book to Malcolm, only the book is not so much about Africa as it is about the woman's coming to terms with her own criminal personality."

I said, "I couldn't put down the John Le Carré, Molly. I couldn't go to sleep until I had finished it."

Molly said, "I am still sitting here at my desk. I am still sorting through all my papers. I won't go to sleep until I have finished and until I find the interview with Matisse, Lily."

I said, "I know what you mean, Molly. I am wide awake now myself. My God, I'll never go back to sleep again just thinking about Inez and the last time I saw her—when was this exactly? The last time I saw Inez was the time we played mah-jong and the time Kevin was shouting at us, which must have been right after I had met Leonard."

Molly said, "The last day, the day I had lunch with Inez —the day I told you about, the day it was raining and Inez kept me waiting—was the day we put the house on the market. I know, I called Bibi that morning to tell her about it."

I said, "The first time I went out with Leonard we went to the seafood restaurant Nora is always talking about, the one she said the United Nations Ambassador from Bolivia always goes to. Molly, are you listening to me? Molly?"

Molly said, "Yes—which seafood restaurant, Lily? The one Claude-Marie said he won't eat at any more? The one Claude-Marie said the last time he ate there he got food poisoning and the one Nora said the only reason she still goes there is it's convenient?"

I said, "After what happened to me in Mexico, don't speak to me about food poisoning. I am very susceptible. This is the first thing I told Leonard when I met him—this and about the pottery lessons."

Molly said, "I agree with you, Lily. Some people can eat anything. Suzanne said she ate a dog once. A collie. And Claude-Marie, oh, God—during the war—I told you what Claude-Marie ate, Lily. Claude-Marie thought it was rabbit."

I said, "Molly, please, please. Let's change the subject, please. I can't bear sad animal stories. I told you about Jason, didn't I? Let's talk about something else. Because what was I saying? Oh, I was telling you about the seafood restaurant and how afterwards I told Nora: But the filet of sole was delicious, and Nora said how the Bolivian ambassador was really a harmless old letch. The Bolivian ambassador to the United Nations, Nora said, had a habit of always putting his hand on her knee while she was translating but he did not mean anything by this. Nora said that now she understood this but not at the beginning, not the first time, and not while she was translating the Diaspora speech for the Palestinians. Nora said she got so flustered she could not remember the word for diaspora in Spanish."

Molly said, "Ha, ha, the same thing happened to me. There must be a word for this. Diaspora is like penis—the word in French, I mean. The word in French is like the word in English, but I didn't know this when I went to see that endless Paul Claudel play about the lost slipper and the man sitting next to me exposed himself. I was also very young then. I was only eighteen, and I did all these things I wouldn't do now— I went swimming, Lily. Can you believe this? I told you, it was a warm day, and I went swimming in my underwear in Matisse's swimming pool—"

I said, "I told you, my mother swam nude. My mother— bless her heart—always swam nude in Martha's Vineyard, and in Nicaragua, too, Leslie said, the beaches are completely deserted. She and Victor never once put on their bathing suits."

Molly said, "I went swimming in only my underwear, Lily, and this is the trouble, Lily, with being so flat-chested, I can never find a bathing suit that fits me—oh, but it's all coming back to me—the French-Canadian journalist said no, he wouldn't, and Matisse, I remember, said if only he was twenty years younger, if only he could get out of the wheelchair. I tell you, Lily, Matisse was a real sport and Matisse was really old by then. How old was Henri Matisse when he died, Lily, do you remember? If only I could find the interview—the interview would say. The interview has all this information—what year Matisse was born, when Matisse first started to paint, etcetera."

I said, "This reminds me—I should call Leslie. Call Leslie about her wedding—oh, how long do you suppose we have been talking on the phone? And what if Claude-Marie is trying to call—remember the story of Inez's father yanking the phone out of the wall while Inez's mother was talking to someone? God—Inez too, could talk for hours. Inez had this extra long extension cord."

Molly said, "When Yuri first moved to Paris and when Yuri still did not have a phone—in France, sometimes you have to wait a whole year to get a telephone installed—Yuri used to come over to the house on rue Madame to call his family in Russia. Oh, God, Lily, you can imagine—Yuri would talk for hours to his mother and to someone called Tanya."

I said, "Don't tell me—from Marrakesh, Sam tried to call the American Express Company the time he was pickpocketed. Sam was trying to bargain the man down—the man was asking a fortune for it, and I don't know how many times I told Sam: Don't put your wallet in your back pocket. Also, I remember, there was this boy with a falcon, and something was wrong with the boy's arm—the arm with the falcon on it. The arm was a bit crooked—deformed, I guess. I felt sorry for the boy, Molly. A nice-looking boy, a boy of around eleven or twelve. I asked the boy what his name was. He said his name was Mohammed. Everyone in Marrakesh was called Mohammed, Molly, all the waiters in the hotel, all the—and like who-do-you-call-it the Spanish boy Inez slept with—Jesus. Jesus Ramirez. Anyhow, and I only thought of this later, Molly, how this boy, this Mohammed, kept hanging around while Sam was bargaining for the rug and how Mohammed kept after us to hold the falcon for money. Mohammed, I remember, wore a glove—a thick leather glove. I took a photo of him. I should show it to you one day. Just a snapshot, but the colors came out nicely—oh, no, nothing like Felicia's photographs. Felicia—don't forget— is a professional photographer, and now, looking back, I wonder if Mohammed did not have something to do with Sam's wallet. Sam had over five hundred dollars in cash in his back pocket and I don't know how many times I told Sam to get travelers' checks."

Molly said, "Oh, please don't talk to me about five hundred dollars. I told Claude-Marie: I will feel a lot better after we sell this house in Connecticut and after we send Bibi away to camp."

I said, "Wait, you didn't let me finish—you didn't hear the rest of what happened to Sam. Sam kept his credit cards in his wallet, his driver's license—his I don't know what all—and when we got back to Cincinnati, we found out someone had charged a truck on Sam's American Express card."

Molly said, "A what, Lily? Hello—can you speak louder? I can't hear you all of a sudden."

I said, "Hello, Molly—a Toyota truck, Molly. But since Sam had telephoned, and since Sam had reported his card stolen, Sam was not held liable. Sam was not responsible. Anyway, I think you are only responsible for the first fifty dollars. The truck cost a lot more. I don't remember the exact figure, but I do remember Sam said it must have been a second-hand vehicle."

Molly said, "Fred has a Toyota pick-up truck and Fred says, so far, his Toyota pick-up is reliable. He is going to drive me to the dentist in it—but speaking of cars, I was just thinking, Lily, how the blue book value of our car is not what we expected it to be, and how it probably means a car without a smashed fender—oh, and, Lily, I also cannot help thinking about Claude-Marie. Whether Claude-Marie found a parking place or whether Claude-Marie put the car in the garage over-night. I should have asked Claude-Marie, Lily, when he telephoned only we got to talking about something else—oh, about Inez—and I forgot to mention this. But Claude-Marie, I remember, said the parking in front of the morgue was no problem whatsoever, which was a small blessing, he said."

I said, "Oh, God, the morgue. I forgot. Where is the morgue? Is the morgue all the way downtown, Molly?"

Molly said, "Price told Claude-Marie how to get there. Price gave Claude-Marie the directions—directions from the West Side Highway, Lily. Normally, Claude-Marie, I told Price, goes down the East River Drive."

I said, "I always take the Triborough Bridge. I don't care what the Triborough costs me because you hear terrible stories, Molly. Stories of people forcing open your car door and grabbing your purse, stories like the one in the book Nora said that she was reading and that she could not put down—the best seller, the same book about which she said—I'll never forget this—thank God, she was reading it on the train and thank God, the book was not in her suitcase. Each day, I swear, life in the city gets more dangerous—what did I hear the other day? A woman was dragged to death by her shoulder bag right here on Park Avenue. No wonder, I told Leonard. I said: A woman alone in the city. No wonder, Inez said she had given up hope. No wonder she let the phone ring and ring and ring and she only answered it at the last minute. It was Kevin. Poor Inez. Inez said she knew the moment Kevin spoke."

Molly said, "Oh, did I tell you how Nora who was watching the commercial for coffee with me said they must have dubbed in Kevin's voice? I told Nora I hated the way Kevin licked his lips pretending the coffee was ice cream, and Nora said, I should have been there to see how Yuri ate the lobsters and how he cracked the shells with his fingers."

I said, "But Molly, you didn't hear how Kevin shouted at us about the damn clack-clacking, you didn't hear him say how he was going to throw out the mah-jong set. And Kevin did not have a stitch on. Kevin, I swear to you, Molly, stood in the doorway in what my mother—bless her heart—called his birthday suit—oh, and did I tell you how this expression never failed to irritate my father? My father would tell my mother: Helen, for God's sakes, there is an old Chinese saying that says: If it is one, then say one, so do me a favor and say *naked*, but what was I saying? Oh—Kevin's Texas accent."

Molly said, "I told you what Claude-Marie said on the phone, didn't I? Claude-Marie said Kevin's clothes were all in the garbage. His T-shirts, his dress shirt with French cuffs, and his toilet kit with everything in it—the electric razor, the toothbrush, the condoms—and Fiddle, I told you, wore gloves, only thank God, Claude-Marie said, Price did not throw out the tuxedo. The tuxedo, Claude-Marie said, was somebody else's tuxedo."

I said, "Molly, the nudity was not what I was talking about. The nudity did not bother me. After all, don't forget, I have seen plenty of naked men. Sam never wore anything. Sam never wore clothes in the house. Sam always ran around naked and this reminds me of one time—have I told you this? Sam was picking up the newspaper off the floor in the front hall and the apartment door slammed shut behind him. This was in Cincinnati, Molly—I was out. Sam had to ring the neighbor's bell to ask if he could borrow something to wear so he could go downstairs and find the superintendent. The poor woman slammed the door in Sam's face. Sam spent a half an hour shouting at her through the closed door, trying to convince her that he was not a rapist and that he lived in the apartment down the hall from hers, only she did not recognize him without his clothes on. I wish I had been there to see this, Molly. It makes me laugh out loud each time I think about this—ha, ha. Men look ridiculous naked, men with their dangling you-know-whats. Sam said he was finally able to convince the woman. He said he told the woman to just throw the pink wrapper on the floor in the hall. You never met Sam, Molly, did you? You met Jim."

Molly said, "I—no—I—hello?"

I said, "Yes—hello—Sam was different. Some people said Sam looked just like Jack Kennedy. In the street, people stopped, people stared at him. Frankly, I never saw the resemblance. Quite honestly, I like Leonard's looks a lot better."

Molly said, "The French count was not what you would

call classically handsome, either. The French count was dark, Lily. Dark hair, dark skin."

I said, "I know what you mean. I said the very same thing, Molly. I said: If Sam looks like Jack Kennedy, then I look like Kate Smith. Because I saw him. Yes, I did. I saw Jack Kennedy in Italy, Molly. Jack Kennedy was standing by that fountain —you know, the fountain if you throw in a coin—the Fontana di Trevi. And Jack Kennedy was not yet president. Jack Kennedy was still a senator. We made eye contact. Jackie was not with him—I was standing right next to him. Oh."

Molly said, "What?"

I said, "Nothing—I was just thinking."

Molly said, "Thinking about what, Lily?"

I said, "Speaking of Jack Kennedy—"

Molly said, "Oh, yes, Jack Kennedy."

I said, "This must be some kind of anniversary—an anniversary of the year of his death, and you know what I was watching last night? I just happened to turn it on—a rerun of the film that showed how Jack Kennedy slumped down on to Jackie's shoulder and how she crawled on her hands and knees in her pink Chanel suit on top of the limousine to get the Secret Service agent to help her."

Molly said, "It's amazing how everyone is always still talking about how they remember exactly where they were and what they were doing on that day."

I said, "I'll never forget, I had just bought Jason—Jason, the dog, Molly—I was on my way home from David Cutler's house—David Cutler raised Labs in Cincinnati, he started this as a hobby, Molly—and I heard the news on the car radio."

Molly said, "I was already in France. I was already sound asleep. But I will always remember what Harry said—Harry,

Suzanne's husband, the lawyer, the litigator. Harry said, this film clip is the most studied film clip in all of history. People have spent more time, Harry said, studying this film clip than they have studying the Dead Sea Scrolls."

I said, "I nearly went off the road when I heard this on the radio. People turned on their headlights, people started honking their horns, and there was poor little Jason whimpering in the back seat. He couldn't have been more than six weeks old. He was just weaned then. The cutest little golden Labrador you have ever seen, Molly. And you know something else, Molly—this is weird. I had planned to call Jason Jack. This is true, swear to God—Jack. Jack is a good name for a dog. Everyone says you should name a dog a one-syllable name, a name you can say quickly like 'Here, boy. Here, Jack.' But after what happened, I couldn't do this. Sam named him. Sam thought up Jason later."

Molly said, "The man who took the film, Lily, was just someone who happened to be standing there watching the motorcade. He was not a professional photographer like Felicia is—oh, and it was because of him that Price shouted and Inez left the dinner table in Old Saybrook."

I said, "Oh, God, you don't have to tell me—I told you how Kevin shouted at us. Sam, too, was always shouting—you should have heard how Sam would shout at the dog. It's a wonder Jason ever obeyed him. I kept telling Sam: *Ja-son* is a two syllable name."

Molly said, "Price, I remember, said how Inez had read every article about Jackie Kennedy at least twice, how Inez knew every item down to the last jodhpur boot in Jackie's closet by heart. The last straw, Price said, was how Inez said she also wanted to take riding lessons. Riding lessons on the money he made? Riding lessons in Central Park at sixty-five dollars an hour? This was what Price had shouted, and I told Inez: Never mind, I'll take you riding. I know a stable in Old Saybrook that only charges you twenty dollars an hour."

I said, "What is the man's name? The man who took the film clip. The name is on the tip of my tongue—I'll think of it in a minute. An odd name, a name like Fiddle's. He must have had a lot of presence of mind, unless, of course, he did not realize what was happening. In a way—Molly, you used to be a photographer—pushing a shutter release—click—and pulling a trigger are similar actions."

Molly said, "I have only shot a gun once in my life, Lily. A shotgun. A twenty-gauge at some doves, and I have always regretted the shot. They say doves are monogamous. Doves mate for life. But the picture I took of Matisse, Lily, was different. The picture I took of Matisse, I would say, was more of an accident. I took it with an old-fashioned Brownie camera. The camera my mother gave me as a goodbye present before I set sail on the *Queen Mary*."

I said, "This opens the door to all kinds of questions—questions of ethics, Molly. Remember the news cameraman who took the pictures of the woman immolating herself, and everyone said that instead, he should have tried to stop her from pouring the gasoline all over herself? But where, I ask you, does one draw the line?"

Molly said, "All I know, Lily, is when I took Matisse's picture, at first Matisse said he was reluctant. Matisse said he was too old for photographs. He said there were plenty of photographs of him already. I had to convince Matisse to let me. I had to tell Matisse I was only an amateur and not a professional. The Brownie camera helped. The camera looked like a lunch box. Also, and to be honest with you, Lily— Matisse, I think, liked me. I told you, didn't I, Lily, how I was just wearing blue jeans and how I went swimming in my underwear in Matisse's swimming pool?"

I said, "The only famous artist, Molly, I ever got to meet was the one with the big mustache—Dali—except I didn't really get to meet Dali, either. Salvador Dali. In Barcelona. Dali was eating dinner at the next table from us in a restaurant and Jim leaned over and asked Dali what it was he was eating and whether Dali would recommend it to us. But what I told Jim—I whispered this to Jim, I didn't want Dali to overhear me—I don't care who it is who is eating those fried eels— Michelangelo, Rembrandt, Picasso—I'm going to order the roast chicken."

Molly said, "Oh, I love Barcelona. I love Gaudi."

I said, "I could not eat the roast chicken, either. The chicken was inedible. This was when we drove to France, Molly. The roads, too, were just terrible. Potholes. Jim said he did not want to stay on the highways. Jim said he liked to take the by-ways. Jim said the by-ways were the only way to see the country and he did not care how long it took us. The best meal we had on that trip, I remember, was in this small restaurant. What was it we ate? Not a *paella* again. A restaurant which wasn't really a restaurant and where there was only room for a couple of people, like in someone's house, where the wife cooked and the husband served and poured the wine. A Marques de Riscal. I don't remember the year, and someone— not Dali, I would have remembered if it had been Salvador Dali—must have recommended this restaurant to us, which was right outside of Toledo—just before you get to Toledo if you are going north, say, the way we were from Barcelona, Molly, and—oh, oh, oh, I just thought of this! I just thought of this right this minute! Oh, and I should have asked her— asked Inez! Molly, maybe this restaurant was in the same village Inez spent the year in, the year Price got the grant. The year Inez said Spain was a mistake because of Jesus Ramirez, and Price said he threw out everything he painted— oh, and wouldn't this have been a coincidence, Molly? Oh, just think about this for a minute. Maybe I did see her—Inez. Maybe our paths crossed in the street. Steep little cobblestone streets. I remember, I remarked on them to Jim. Very picturesque, I said. I said, if I had a camera I would take a picture of them. But, of course, I was not carrying anything—no, not like Inez. Only my purse, I guess. I know I would never have left my purse with my money and my passport in the car. The car was rented. A Renault."

Molly said, "Oh, I love Madrid. I love El Greco."

I said, "The restaurant was called something *del Sol.* Hello—Molly, are you awake?"

Molly said, "Yes, yes, Lily—what time is it? It must be after four in the morning. If I called up Bibi, Bibi would have eaten breakfast by now, and Bibi would have gone off to school with Jerome and Véronique—only Bibi does not eat breakfast any more. I told you, didn't I, Lily, how Bibi is almost taller than I am and how Bibi only weighs forty-five kilos?"

I said, "How much does Bibi weigh, Molly?"

Molly said, "You have to multiply a kilo by two point two to get what Bibi weighs in pounds, Lily. I hate all those conversions and I can never figure out how many kilometers in a mile and how to change Centigrade into Fahrenheit."

I said, "All I know is that it is only about fifty degrees out now—oh, but this also reminds me of the time I was in Italy and I bought an ice cream. I had a what-do-you-call-it *gelati* the day I visited the fountain you throw your money into, the day Jack Kennedy smiled at me and we made eye contact, and this single scoop of *gelati*, Molly, cost me thousands of lire.

Oh, and when I bought the dress—the blue dress with the gold flecks in it, the dress I might wear to Leslie's wedding—I completely lost track of the zeros."

Molly said, "Now I have it, Lily. Bibi weighs ninety-nine pounds. Bibi weighs less than one hundred pounds."

I said, "I remember, I told Sam: I don't care if your wallet was stolen, I am still going to buy the dress. Well-made clothes last forever."

Molly said, "Claude-Marie, too, has clothes from since he was a boy and from before the war, the Second World War —oh, and poor Claude-Marie. When Price called, Claude-Marie was in his pajamas already, he had to get dressed again, and I told Claude-Marie: Look at me, I am not in bed yet, I am still sorting through these papers in my desk—I told you, tomorrow I have to go to the dentist."

I said, "You are right, Molly—someone had to go and where, I ask you, would any of us be if no one ever did anything? Where I ask you would we be if no one took a stand—a stand against the greenhouse effect, a stand against the deforestation of the Amazon, and what about pollution? Acid rain? The ozone layer—oh, remember how Inez used to worry about the ozone layer? What did Inez say? Inez said: Me and my fine skin, I'm just kidding—oh, and what else—drugs? Yes, the war on drugs. And what was it I read in the paper the other day? I read about an asteroid orbiting around the sun at forty-six thousand miles an hour that just missed hitting us. The asteroid missed the earth by a half a million miles. Imagine, Molly—in cosmic terms, a half a million miles is next to nothing. The astronomer whom they interviewed said: Yes, yes. Sooner or later. Now this, I said, is something to worry about. And this, Malcolm said, proved his theory—his second moon theory. Sixty-five million years ago, Malcolm said, an asteroid fell into the ocean and caused a huge tidal wave, which destroyed Atlantis and killed off all the dinosaurs. Remember, Molly? Weren't you there when Malcolm said this? When Malcolm showed us the rubbings? The Inca rubbings Malcolm brought all the way from his house in East Hampton to show Price. You can ask him. Ask Price."

Molly said, "Malcolm has all kinds of funny theories. It was Malcolm, remember, who told us about this idea he had for a new kind of museum, Lily. A scent museum, a museum to preserve smells. Smells that you might want to keep, smells that might no longer exist and might also become extinct—the smell of baking bread, for instance, or the smell of old-fashioned roses, or of cigarette smoke, and everyone at the restaurant—the Vietnamese restaurant—when Malcolm told us this, made rude noises. Remember—Yuri farted."

I said, "Oh, Yuri—he did? At will? Yuri is something. But I remember Jason—the dog—used to do this in the car. I would have to open all the windows, even in the winter. Winter in Cincinnati—ugh. The roads from our house were sheer ice. I would tell Sam: I, for one, am not going to drive on this stuff. I, for one, am not going to land in the hospital."

Molly said, "Oh, God, don't remind me about Bibi and Jerome on the motorcycle, because the last time I spoke to Bibi I wanted to ask her if she finally had made up her mind about this summer and instead, all Bibi could talk about was a test. A biology test she had failed, Bibi said, and that Jerome, who had not studied for it half as much as Bibi said she had, got a hundred on."

I said, "Oh—I nearly flunked biology, Molly. Our teacher, Mrs. Millard, I'll never forget, was a real martinet. She was also very overweight and one day, Mrs. Millard perched herself on top of one of the stools to dissect something and the stool gave way. Mrs. Millard hit her head against the radiator. How can I forget this? The whole class was excused, and we all rushed off to the movies."

Molly said, "But Mrs. Millard? She didn't die, did she?"

I said, "Mrs. Millard? No. She died later. She died of something else. They named the school lab after her. The Eleanor Mosby Millard Laboratory, which sounds very grand when all it was was a couple of rusty Bunsen burners—oh, and, Molly, I still remember the movie we went to."

Molly said, "The first school I ever went to, Lily, the teacher rang a bell. All the children from first grade through sixth grade studied together. The schoolhouse too, was painted red, and I'll never forget what we nicknamed the teacher. We probably did not know what vagina meant. Kids then were not as sophisticated as kids are today—kids like Jerome and Bibi, I mean."

I said, "We saw *East of Eden*."

Molly said, "Oh, with James Dean."

I said, "Julie Harris was in it, too. Remember how the two of them kissed on the Ferris wheel? —but what were we talking about, Molly?"

Molly said, "Bibi—poor Bibi flunking her biology test."

I said, "At least Bibi is getting an education. Nowadays, all you hear on television is how badly educated American kids are—oh, and what was the word you used, Molly? Not *palimpsest*, the other one? *Innumerate*. Yes, how innumerate the kids today are. One of the kids I heard said he thought Chernobyl was Cher's real name and the District of Columbia, he said, was some place in Central America. Makes you think, doesn't it? I watched this program the night I was supposed to play bridge with Nora and Nora could not make it. Remember, Nora said she had a problem with her sister, Mercedes, and

I said: For heaven's sake, Nora, Mercedes is not a problem. I told Nora we could take turns, we could each sit out a hand, and Nora said the problem was Mercedes had a stomach ache."

Molly said, "Yes, if only Mercedes had rented Inez's room, things, Lily, could have been different."

I said, "But Nora was lucky. That night, Mercedes had to have an emergency appendectomy—poor Mercedes. I told Nora: If Mercedes has to stay in the hospital a long time, I'll—oh, this reminds me, Molly, of what Sam said if something should happen. Sam said we should have our appendices out before we crossed the Sahara, and I told Sam to go ahead and have his out if he wanted to, I was more concerned about running out of gas or getting lost in the desert."

Molly said, "I just remembered—Regina Pendleton was my teacher's name. I wonder what has happened to poor old Regina. Regina would be in her eighties now, and you know something else, Lily, to this day, I feel guilty—oh, and what time did you say it was?"

I said, "That's the thing, time goes by so quickly, and what did you say, Molly? What time is it? It's after four-thirty in the morning, but I was telling you what I told Sam—any operation that requires anesthetic involves a certain risk, this is what my brother William said—William is a surgeon, Molly, an orthopedic surgeon—and a little girl, God forbid she was a patient of William's, died right there in Richmond while she was having her tonsils out. The little girl, William said, got an infection. The infection must have spread through the radiators and this affected a lot of other people in that hospital. People who were just in there for routine surgery or to have babies."

Molly said, "Oh, I was lucky with Bibi. Bibi was easy. Only some people—Inez, for instance—Inez was in labor for thirty-six hours before they had to do a Caesarean on her. And just look at fifty or sixty years ago, look at a hundred years ago, look at Emily Dickinson—then half the women died in child-birth or of pneumonia."

I said, "Molly, I had pneumonia. I caught pneumonia from living in that apartment with no hot water—remember the apartment overlooking the Parc Monceau? Every time I turned on the shower, Molly, the water came out freezing cold, and when I complained to the landlord—Monsieur Gruass was his name—Monsieur Gruass would start on this same long harangue about how during the war he never had a hot bath, how Americans were too soft and too spoilt, how Americans had never endured any of the hardships their allies had, and, Molly, on and on and blah, blah, blah, he said, and Monsieur Gruass would corner me. Monsieur Gruass would corner me on the stairs, he would block the steps so I couldn't go up or so I couldn't go down and until I would end up thinking: A freezing cold shower is better any day than having to listen to this old windbag. Poor Monsieur Gruass. He died, Molly. Monsieur Gruass died on the bus. The number ninety-two bus went to the end of the line—who knows where this was —Neuilly? Boulogne Billancourt? No one noticed, and not until the bus driver turned around and said something like: *Nous voilà* or *Nous sommes arrivés*, and by then Monsieur Gruass had turned blue already."

Molly said, "The war, I know. Claude-Marie starts all of his sentences with: During the war when I was a boy—or: When I was a boy during the war—and I say to him: Enough, Claude-Marie. I say to Claude-Marie: I don't want to hear one more time how during the war, you, Claude-Marie, could not buy a pair of shoes or how you, Claude-Marie, had to eat rabbits and how, one time, your mother did not say the rabbit was a cat and what made you so sick to your stomach."

I said, "Everywhere—not just in France, Molly, people had

to make do. My mother—bless her heart—who was pregnant with me at the time, said that sugar was rationed and that she had a craving for candy. To the day she died, Molly, whenever she went out or whenever my mother went to a restaurant, my mother would take some sugar cubes home with her. She would put the sugar cubes in her purse. Just in case, she always said. In case of what? I would tease her. In case you get pregnant?"

Molly said, "Oh—sugar always reminds me of the count, Lily. Of a story he told me—"

I said, "You mean how sugar expands, Molly? Everyone knows that story and how, at last, someone figured out to make a little slit in the paper wrapper."

Molly said, "No, this story is about a cement mixer, Lily, a cement mixer truck if it gets stuck. The French count told me the only way to keep the cement from hardening inside the truck is to pour sugar in—*des centaines de kilo de sucre* was what the count said to me."

I said, "I told you, Molly, I've forgotten most of my French. Anyway, who was it who said the best way to learn a new language is to have a lover teach you? Yuri probably."

Molly said, "No, not Yuri, Lily—Yuri cannot speak a single language properly—and what did Claude-Marie say the other day about Yuri's new girlfriend? Claude-Marie said: *L'amie de Yuri est très jolie et elle est indochinoise mais franchement, jamais je n'arriverai à prononcer son nom.*"

I said, "Oh, dear, Leonard doesn't speak French either. Leonard only speaks English. But I wonder, Molly, whether my decision was too quick—my decision about Leonard's mother, I mean. I told you Leonard's mother lives in Maryland. Leonard's mother lives in a town not far from Washington and right off the Beltway, and I told Leonard that

Maryland is too hot in the summer. I said I would rather go and visit his mother in September."

Molly said, "No, no, you're right, Lily. Virginia, too, is terrible in June. Not just the heat, the humidity. I'll always remember, Lily, how during the Miss Marys' summer solstice recital everyone, including my own mother and father, sat there dripping sweat and listening to those poems by the Rossettis, and I remember, too, how one time someone in the audience passed out and fell out of his chair and Miss Mary kept right on going, Miss Mary never wavered: *The blessed damozel leaned out/From the gold bar of Heaven.*"

I said, "Oh, I can still remember my lines from *Julius Caesar.* I played Marc Antony, Molly. *Friends, Romans, countrymen, lend me your ears;/ I come to bury Caesar, not to praise him./ The evil that men do lives after them;/ the good is oft interred with their bones./ So let it be with Caesar*—Molly? Are you listening to this?"

Molly said, "I am, Lily. I am listening to every word. I am just trying to remember what came after: *Her eyes were deeper than the depth/Of waters* or something-or-other like this. Then *She had three lilies in her hand/And the stars in her hair were seven.*"

I said, "Molly, you should have seen me. I wore this white tunic that kept slipping off my shoulders, I carried a sword made out of papier-mâché. *If you have tears, prepare to shed them now*—remember this? My favorite lines were: *There is a tide in the affairs of men/ Which taken at the flood, leads on to fortune;/ Omitted, all the voyage of their life/ Is bound in shallows and miseries.* Also, I will never forget the girl who played Brutus. Her name was Anne—Anne with an E. God forbid anyone should forget the E. I loathed her. Anne was so competitive. Anne was captain of the volleyball team."

Molly said, "I am still trying to remember who it was who fainted and fell out of his chair during Miss Mary's recital."

I said, "Oh—Zapruder, Molly! Zapruder is the man's name who shot the film of Kennedy's assassination. The whole time we were talking I have been trying to think of it. I went through the entire alphabet beginning with A in my head."

Molly said, "Yes, I hate not to remember something and I hate not to find something. I told you how I am still looking for the interview—the interview with Matisse. I promised Havier I would show it to him. Matisse, Havier told me, is his favorite Impressionist."

I said, "Van Gogh is my favorite artist. How many millions was the last van Gogh painting sold for, Molly?"

Molly said, "I told you how if only Claude-Marie had not followed Thomas Hamlin Aldrich's investment advice and how if only—but let's not talk about money, Lily. Claude-Marie said: Money is not everything, and I should take a good look at Madame Florisson's daughter-in-law. Who would have guessed? Now, Claude-Marie said, Madame Florisson's daughter-in-law has a brand-new lease on life. The last time he saw her, Claude-Marie said, Madame Florisson's daughter-in-law was all decked out in a brand-new mini-skirt. Everyone in Paris, I told Claude-Marie, is wearing those things now. Soon, I said, if we are not careful, Bibi will be. Or Bibi will be wearing those skin-tight things people go running or bicycling in, like what Ngh, Yuri's new girlfriend, wears—the girlfriend with the unpronounceable name—which is another reason why I told Claude-Marie I hope Bibi changes her mind and goes to camp this summer."

I said, "Molly, send Bibi to the camp in Maine I went to, the same camp I told Inez she should have sent her boys to, the time I told Inez: You never know—this was when I told

Inez how my father survived the terrible squall by treading water and hanging on to the hull of the boat, and Inez told me but she didn't know how to swim anyway."

Molly said, "Wasn't your father wearing a life-vest? Suzanne said when she crossed the Atlantic in the small sailboat—the ketch, the time she gave up cigarettes—she never once took off her life-vest. Suzanne said she kept her life-vest on to do everything—even to go to the bathroom, she said, only Suzanne called it the head. Suzanne said she also kept on her life-vest the one time the wind died down enough for her and Harry to make love."

I said, "Isn't this something? Roberta told me she made love in the lavatory of an airplane once. Frankly, I do not care what Roberta does. I told Roberta: There isn't even room enough to wash your hands in there, which was also what I told Inez. I told Inez: I don't care how many times you and Kevin make love. Sex is not the answer to everything."

Molly said, "Exactly what I have said to Bibi, Lily."

I said, "And I said: Inez, I am not frigid. I told Inez she could ask Leonard. She could ask Jim. She could ask a number of people. I told Inez: The first boy I slept with was when I was seventeen years old. I'll never forget him. Peter wrote me these long letters—I almost wish I had kept them—letters he wrote me while he was working for this construction company way up north near Juneau, Alaska. Peter wrote how he had to live in a barrack with hundreds of other men—Poles mostly, Czechs. Men, Peter said, who did not speak English, and men who drank a lot and who fought each other with knives. If only I had kept them I could read you those letters, Molly. The letters sort of reminded me of how what's-his-name the writer who wrote about people freezing to death in the snow and who wrote about huskies—oh, of how Jack London wrote.

The letters were sort of a mixture between Jack London and Hemingway—oh, my father, Molly, knew Ernest Hemingway, only this is a whole other story—and I wrote Peter and I told Peter: You could be just like a writer, you could be just like Hemingway. I don't know what became of Peter, but I'll never forget how, in one of his letters, Peter wrote about this one young man, a Pole, I guess, who drove his huge bulldozer off an embankment. The clutch cable broke and the young Pole could not get the bulldozer geared down, and Peter wrote how he and everyone working on the same site could hear the young Pole screaming all the way down the side of the mountain, and, Molly, believe me, Peter wrote this so vividly that to this day and while I am talking to you right this minute on the phone. I can still hear that young Pole screaming."

Molly said, "Oh, horrible—poor man. You should have kept those letters, Lily."

I said, "Some people are naturally born story-tellers—my father was. My father could talk your ear off about Cuba and fishing and sailing and about how he met Hemingway. My father could talk until the cows came home was what my mother—bless her heart—used to say about him. But you're right, Molly, those screams kind of stay with you. And something about a man screaming. It's so poignant."

Molly said, "I told you how the Closerie des Lilas was Hemingway's favorite restaurant, didn't I? I told you how I went there with Price."

I said, "Men scream louder is why. You should have heard Sam—"

Molly said, "Didier. Lily, you should have heard how Didier yelled at me for touching his stamp, the Penny Black. No wonder I told Claude-Marie I wouldn't go to his house for lunch the day the plane crashed."

I said, "I know, you've told me, Molly. But you should

have heard how Sam yelled at the man in the desert—the man who threw the rock through the car windshield. The funny thing was Felicia won a first prize for that picture at an exhibition, and what I told Sam afterwards was: Those judges should have taken a good look at our car. The front seat was nothing but shards of broken glass and Sam was still yelling something about wouldn't-you-know-it-the-goddam-car-picked-this-goddam-moment-to-stall-on-us. Luckily, I was in the back seat with the sandwiches—the sandwiches the hotel in Marrakesh had fixed for our lunch."

Molly said, "Oh, Dominique, too—this was what Dominique said. She said she spent the whole day fixing lunch for us. Dominique said she spent the whole day in the kitchen cooking this huge meal—a leg of lamb, potatoes—although Dominique knows perfectly well Claude-Marie won't eat potatoes — and all kinds of vegetables. A dessert, too. Dominique said she made *tirami su*. I tell you, Lily, if I heard about this *tirami su* once, I heard about *tirami su* a dozen times."

I said, "Oh—*tirami su*. *Tirami su* is Leonard's favorite dessert. A kind of runny pudding, isn't it? I tasted Leonard's the other night. Leonard said the *tirami su* I tasted was not as good as it should have been and for me to stay open-minded about it. Hello? Hello, Molly? Are you there? The other funny thing and you may not believe this, but I had never heard of *tirami su* before in my life. No, I swear to you, Molly, never. And now, of course, I am hearing about *tirami su* all the time, which is like what we were saying just now."

Molly said, "Yum—this also reminds me of Madame Florisson's lemon tart. All this talk about food is making me hungry. Did I tell you I did not have any supper? I told Claude-Marie: Best to pick up something to eat on the road—a hamburger or a hot dog."

I said, "I had filet of sole for supper, and Leonard, to begin with, had oysters. I told Leonard: No, no, I'm not allergic, thank you, then I told Leonard how my father nearly choked to death in a restaurant. My father scared the life out of me, I said. My father turned bright red, then he turned ash white. I thought my father was having a heart attack. Like Monsieur Gruass on the bus. Thank God for the waiter is what I said. Thank God, the waiter had the presence of mind. The waiter grabbed my father right under the ribs and the oyster shot out of my father's mouth and landed across the table right in my lap. I swear, Molly, this is true. This was what I told Leonard, too."

Molly said, "Lily, I know, I know. Oysters and shellfish are poison."

I said, "This is what I said to Leslie: Don't serve shrimp at your wedding."

Molly said, "Yes, except soon it's going to be light and it's still raining out—and what did I tell you? I told you I have no sense of time. My God, I have no idea how long we've been talking on the phone, Lily."

I said, "Molly — hours. My mother—bless her heart—my mother was just like this. My mother was always late."

Molly said, "I told you—Inez, too, was late. Inez kept me waiting for nearly an hour the day we had lunch together."

I said, "My mother was always late for everything. The time I was just telling you about, Molly, when my father nearly choked to death on the oyster, my mother had not arrived at the restaurant yet. My mother—bless her heart—only got there afterwards. She said she could not understand what all the fuss was about and why we had to leave such a big tip for the waiter. And what else did my mother say? My father, my mother said—and she said she was not even talking about the overturned boat—was accident-prone. So was William, my brother, Molly. No wonder, William is an orthopedic surgeon, William spent his whole adolescence on crutches or wearing a cast—oh, oh, this reminds me of something—something William said he saw as part of the tour when he went to China with the group of doctors and Lucille, his wife, was included. William said he saw this operation, and the operation had something to do with—of course—acupuncture. An operation on a boy, Molly—are you listening to me? You will never believe this. No. A Chinese boy who had lost both his legs in a train accident and the Chinese doctors, William said— William was watching the whole thing, and I would also be amazed, was what William said, at how he and the other doctors did not have to wear surgical gowns and how they were just standing around watching the operation in their street clothes —and the Chinese doctors, William said, had managed to save part of one leg and attach this leg back to what was left of the other leg, not the same leg, Molly, the *other* leg, and later—Molly, you won't believe this—the boy wiggled his toes for them to show that the operation had been a success— incredible, isn't it?"

Molly said, "Lily, I believe everything. You should have seen Madame Florisson's daughter-in-law. Madame Florisson's daughter-in-law, Claude-Marie said, was literally at death's door a few short months ago."

I said, "When I asked Lucille—Lucille is William's wife, William's second wife—Lucille said that seeing the operation had been optional, and that she, Lucille said, had chosen to visit the Forbidden City instead. Lucille said she visited the Forbidden City the same day Henry and Nancy Kissinger did—no, no, not the time Kissinger went there with Nixon, another time, later—and I told Lucille how I had run into Jack Kennedy at the Fontana di Trevi in Italy. I told Lucille how running into Kissinger would not have given me a very big thrill—which reminds me of a stupid joke—have you heard this one, Molly? The next time I talk to Lucille I should tell her—a young man makes an appointment to see Henry Kissinger at his new consulting firm and the young man asks Kissinger: Dr. Kissinger, is it true that you charge twenty thousand dollars for each question? And Kissinger answers him: Yah, jung man. Vat is your second question?"

Molly said, "Twenty thousand dollars? Yikes. What would I ever want to ask Kissinger, anyway? Dr. Kissinger, should I get a permanent?"

I said, "Molly—you're not serious. You will ruin your hair, your beautiful hair."

Molly said, "I was just kidding, Lily."

I said, "Okay, I guess the joke wasn't very funny, but go ahead and tell the one you promised, Molly—the horse's dick joke. Oh, I bet I know—is it the one about Twenty Questions and how Queen Elizabeth after only her first question—*Is it edible?*—guesses what is inside the black box? I can never get jokes right. Either I forget or I give away the punch line. There is an art to it, like acting, and when I played Marc Antony and I had to say the speech about *Great Caesar fell./ Oh, what a fall was there, my countrymen!/ Then I, and you and all of us fell down./ Whilst bloody treason flourish'd over us*, I drew a blank. I could not remember. I completely forgot my lines. Now, years later, wouldn't you know it, I remember the lines word for word. I remember the lines perfectly. Actually, knowing things by heart, Molly, can be a great comfort—I don't mean just prayers, I mean poems and Shakespeare. I'll never forget how when we ran out of gas in the desert and Jim had to hitchhike to the nearest town, Jim left me alone in the car for over two hours and it was already dark by then. The reason, Jim said, was someone from the gas station had to drive him back, and since the gas station was a one-man operation, the gas station attendant had to go get his wife to drive Jim back in the tow truck. Oh, and Molly, I will never forget the man's wife. Jim said the whole time she was driving him back she was breast-feeding her child. Jim said she kept one hand on the steering wheel, one hand on the child, the tow truck too, he said, was the old kind. The kind, Jim said, with a clutch and a gear shift."

Molly said, "Oh, yes, I know, our car is exactly like this, Lily. I mean, the car I backed over the cat with, the car Claude-Marie drove into the city with. It's not a whatchamacallit hydromatic, Lily. But I have never been good about cars—and no wonder. Just think of all the accidents I've been in—the accident with the two dogs stuck doing it, the accident with the French count in the Lancia—oh, I nearly forgot—my near-death experience, Lily. The red BMW in the garage in San Anton. Hello? Can you hear me—hello, Lily?"

I said, "Yes, I am here, Molly, and just what I was thinking. I was thinking Leonard has a Volvo."

Molly said, "If only the French count had been driving the Citroën."

I said, "Red too, Molly—red. Statistically, red is the safest color. They have made studies to show how gray blends right into the highway."

Molly said, "The Citroën was black and the Citroën was more comfortable, Lily."

I said, "The only time I drove in Paris, right away I got a ticket. I had not even gotten as far as the *périphérique* yet—I was on my way to visit the chateaus of the Loire Valley, Molly, and Jim, I remember, said he could not come with me—and the policeman told me I had run a red light. I did not dare argue with him, Molly, although I swear to you the light had just turned yellow. The policeman made me pay the ticket right there on the spot—I'll never forget, it cost me two hundred francs. At the time, Molly, the exchange rate was only four francs to the dollar so the ticket cost me fifty dollars, while now the same ticket would only cost me about thirty-five dollars—oh, but what was I saying?"

Molly said, "I've never been to the Loire Valley, Lily, I've never visited Chenonceau or Chambord or Amboise or Blois or Azay-le-Rideau or whatever those chateaus are called. I am not a good sightseer—I told you, I've never been up the Eiffel Tower either, although Bibi has. Bibi, remember, said that from where she was standing, she could see Mademoiselle Boudemange's apartment."

I said, "The time I went up the Eiffel Tower, it was so windy and crowded. The man standing next to me, I remember, nearly lost his hat. His hat nearly got blown away, Molly. The man's wife, or the woman who was with him, kept saying: *Guillaume, fais attention! Ton chapeau. Guillaume, ton chapeau va s'envoler si tu ne fais pas attention. Tu m'entends, Guillaume? Ton chapeau.* This was all the woman kept repeating and saying to him the whole time I was up there. She never once remarked on the view or on anything. She just kept nattering away at him about his hat. But maybe this is love, Molly. Who knows? Anyway, this was what I told Price the time Price was telling me the story about the workman. Remember, Molly? The workman showing off to his girlfriend who fell off the Eiffel Tower, and Inez, who was there while Price was telling the story, said: But, Price, what about the girlfriend? And what if it was at night, did the girlfriend have to climb down by herself in the dark? Or did she have to wait until the next morning, and what if the next morning was a

Sunday?—after all, France is a Catholic country. The girl-friend, poor woman, Inez said, would have had to wait another day, and Price told Inez to be quiet please, to let him please finish, and, after all, this was not the point of the story."

Molly said, "I don't understand. Who said this? Did Inez say all this? Did Inez make all this up?"

I said, "Inez told Price she could not stop thinking about this woman, and what if the workman had just made love to the woman was what Inez said she was asking Price. Inez said she could picture her perfectly, the woman up there alone on top of the Eiffel Tower, the woman wearing a flimsy dress and high heel shoes, red high heel shoes, was what Inez said, and Price got annoyed with her then—with Inez. Price told Inez he did not know what the issue was here and he didn't know what the color of the woman's shoes had to do with any of this, and, yes, of course, the woman, Price told Inez, had to climb down the way she climbed up, the way everyone did before they installed the elevator—the way he did, too—the way, Price said, he climbed to the top of the Eiffel Tower in under an hour the time he came to Paris for his sculpture and the time, he said, he was still in training for the marathon."

Molly said, "The time Price and I had the drink at the Closerie des Lilas, the time the plane crashed. Oh, and here I am, still sorting through my desk. Oh, and Lily, how I wish I could find the interview with Matisse. I would read it to you, Lily—the part where Matisse speaks about his painting, about his art, Lily."

I said, "This reminds me, I should be reading a book for my French conversation club. A book by Guy de Maupassant, Molly."

Molly said, "Guy de Maupassant?—I don't know one thing about him, but I am sure Bibi does."

I said, "Guy de Maupassant's stories are sort of like O'Henry's —you know, with a surprise ending. The story I am reading now reminds me a little of when I borrowed Inez's kimono to go to the Sayonara party for Jim's boss's retirement. I told you, didn't I, how Jim's boss burned a cigarette hole in it and how I spilt *sake* on it? And you know when you drink *sake*, Molly, how they serve it lukewarm in these tiny cups so you can't taste the alcohol and so you don't even know how much *sake* you've drunk and, before you know it, you are drunk. This was also what I told Jim. I told Jim: *Sake* is as lethal as gin, and I don't even remember how we got home from the party, Molly—all I remember was dancing with Jim's boss, who had a cigarette dangling from his mouth, and Jim, too, couldn't remember a thing—oh, and you should have seen what Jim wore. Jim wore these pajamas, black silk pajamas, and Jim wore a coolie hat, and the only trouble, Molly, was Jim's pajama fly had no buttons, the pajama fly was just this string thing and Jim said: It's so damn hot, who cares anyhow whether I am wearing underwear, and I said: Jim, I can see everything—hello, Molly, are you listening?"

Molly said, "Wait—oh, for a minute, I thought I had found it—found the interview with Matisse. No. It's something else. It's the newspaper clipping about the woman who found the hand grenade in with her potatoes—remember? Inez sent it to me. The woman lived in Paris—in Neuilly, it says here. But you're right, Lily, I hate costume parties. I hate to dress up."

I said, "I know—I can't help it. I still can't stop thinking about how I felt the next morning, Molly, when I saw the burn hole and the *sake* stains on Inez's blue-and-white silk kimono. When Jim woke up, I said: Oh, God, tell me what should I do now? How can I ever face Inez again, was what

I said to Jim. I swear to you, Molly, I felt just like the woman in the de Maupassant story, the woman who, like me, borrows something from her best friend—only she borrows a diamond necklace—to go to a dance. And what happens next? You're right—of course. The woman loses the necklace. Then— because the woman is too embarrassed and too ashamed to tell her friend, her best friend—she goes and buys a diamond necklace just like it. Only the necklace the woman buys costs her thousands—thousands of francs, I guess—and the woman has to spend years—the best years of her life, say—working to pay for the necklace. She scrimps and saves and she works all day on her hands and knees scrubbing floors. She ruins her looks, her health too, and years go by until one day, accidentally, she runs into her friend again. At first, the friend does not recognize her, but the woman who lost the necklace decides to confess, to make a clean breast of the whole thing, and to tell her best friend how she lost the diamond necklace at the dance and how, ever since, she has been slaving away to make up for this loss—which, by the way, she says is also the reason why they have not seen each other and why her friend did not recognize her—and the best friend, when she hears all this, says: Oh, but my dear, the necklace was fake. The diamonds were not real. Can you imagine, Molly? I would have killed myself. The waste. Funny, too, when I first read the story, my instinct was to try and fix it. To work out the story some other way and so that the woman right away asks her friend: Was this really a valuable necklace with real dia-monds you lent me that I lost at the dance? I kept trying to have the story come out differently. Molly, Molly, are you listening to me?"

Molly said, "Yes, yes, yes—but you know me, I never get dressed up. I never wear anything but jeans. The last time I went shopping for an evening dress was with Amy. This was when I also said to her: Amy, when will you ever wear a dress like this? But I was wrong, Lily, Amy said she did wear the dress from Miller and Rhoads with the tiny spaghetti straps to the Farmington Hunt Club Ball. Furthermore, Amy said, after the electroshock treatment, the only person she danced with who still looked like a monkey to her was her husband."

I said, "It's like if I were to reread *Gone with the Wind* or *Anna Karenina*, a part of me would still hope that this time around Anna will not fall in love with that cad Vronsky again and that Rhett Butler will give a damn at the end now."

Molly said, "Yes—all I can say is thank God, Lily. Thank God, the woman who found the live hand grenade in her sack of potatoes—the woman in the newspaper clipping—did not pull the pin—Lily?"

I said, "It makes you think, doesn't it? Makes you think about life—which reminds me, Molly, just the other day, I had a real madman at the wheel—the day I took a taxi to see Inez, the day we played mah-jong with the playwright from Sri Lanka and from downstairs. You should have seen him, the taxi driver is who I mean, and if you think I am bad about going through red lights, this man ignored them completely. Red lights simply did not exist for him. He was some sort of Indian. Indian Indian, Molly—he wore a turban. From one of those fanatic sects, I bet. I didn't dare say a word. I was afraid he would turn around and cut my head off. What is it that they are supposed to always carry with them? A knife, a comb?"

Molly said, "Oh, oh, I can hear it, it's raining harder again. I tell you, the woman was lucky, the woman could have pulled the pin, Lily."

I said, "I know. It's just drizzling here—it's not raining the way it rained yesterday, Molly. Yesterday, it poured. On the way home from that seafood place, I told Leonard: Even if I had remembered to bring along an umbrella, I would still rather rent a video of a film—oh, and you know which one Leonard picked?—*My Dinner with André*. Have you seen it, Molly? André Gregory and Wally Shawn are supposed to be discussing the meaning of life while in actual fact, they are stuffing themselves with quail at a fancy New York restaurant. André Gregory says things to Wally Shawn like you don't have to climb Mount Everest to find reality, reality can be found right around the corner in the cigar store on Seventh Avenue—and what else does André Gregory say? You know how he talks in his phony aristocratic foreign accent—'I cood alvays leave in my art and not in my liefe'—and I asked Leonard: What do you suppose he means by that—oh, but why did I mention this? Inez? Was it because of Inez, Molly?"

Molly said, "Yes. Inez. Yes, we were talking about Inez. Poor Inez."

I said, "I still can't believe what you said—said about Inez—that Inez is—Oh, but speaking of accents, Molly—no, no, don't get me wrong, I like Ivan, only I have to concentrate—concentrate on what Ivan says, otherwise—oh, and like the time I asked Nora if, besides her yoga class, she also meditated, and you know what Ivan answered? Before either Nora or I could stop him, Ivan told us this long and involved story about how when he was living in an ashram in India, he saw this Buddhist monk sitting cross-legged, two feet up in the air in the lotus position, holding his bowl and eating his dinner. Ivan said how the monk smacked his lips and ate rice with his chopsticks while all the time he was defying gravity—levitating. Can you believe this?"

Molly said, "Oh, gravity, I know—Ivan exaggerates. All Russians exaggerate. I still can't figure out how on earth Yuri's mother could have known Chekhov."

I said, "You're right, Molly. There is a world of difference between knowing someone and just seeing someone accidentally, for a minute, the way I saw Jack Kennedy—oh, but what was I just thinking? Oh, Inez, and Inez's two boys. I can't stop thinking about them—about Price Junior and Matthew— about Inez's mother too, poor woman. I told you, didn't I, how I met Inez's mother at the birthday party and how Inez's mother said she had to leave early? Inez's mother said how sorry she was to leave before the gorilla sang *Happy Birthday*. Inez's mother said she had to get back to New Jersey. I remember, I asked Inez's mother which of the two tunnels she preferred—Inez's mother told me that most of the time she drove uptown, she took the George Washington Bridge. In the long run, the bridge was quicker, Inez's mother said, and I said I agreed with her. I told Inez's mother how Sam and I once got stuck in the Lincoln Tunnel for forty minutes. I am not exaggerating—in the middle of summer, in July, Molly. I thought I was going to die. Not just the heat. The lack of air—the lack of oxygen. Sam said for me not to open the car window and Sam said for me to relax and to keep breathing. I said to Sam: What if I hyperventilate? Oh, and Jason, the dog, Molly, was sitting in the back seat. Jason was panting so hard, his tongue looked like it was going to fall out of his mouth."

Molly said, "I told you, I don't drive anymore since I ran over the cat, but poor Claude-Marie."

I said, "Oh, but Claude-Marie, Molly, was going the other way. Claude-Marie was going against the traffic. How long did it take Claude-Marie, did Claude-Marie say, Molly? Three hours? Two hours and a half? Wait until Memorial Day, the traffic will get worse then. Last summer when I drove out to Malcolm's house in East Hampton, I spent three hours in bumper-to-bumper traffic and I asked myself: Is a dip in the ocean worth this?"

Molly said, "I love to swim and I told you how I used to drive down from Charlottesville to Nag's Head, North Carolina, to visit Amy, my best friend."

I said, "As a child, I spent the summers I did not go to camp on Martha's Vineyard, and my mother—bless her heart—I told you already, Molly, how my mother would go down to the beach early, before any of us in the house was awake. My mother would swim for an hour by herself and my father would worry about her. My father would say things to her like: Now, Helen, remember your friend Estelle Davidson and remember, if anything happens to you, I told you so and you have no one to blame but yourself. My father always liked to have the last word about everything. Even things he knew nothing about, my father still had to have an opinion. Give him half a chance, my father, I bet, would have told William exactly how to set a broken leg, and my father was not a doctor. My father was very conservative. He could not understand, no matter what the circumstances, why every one couldn't just pull themselves up by his boot straps—his words, Molly —and go to Harvard and make a lot of money the way he had. My father thought the underclass was just lazy. You couldn't argue with him. God knows, I don't blame my mother. In those days people didn't get divorced so easily. My mother probably went swimming by herself to get away from him. And after what happened to my father in the boat, my father always had what he called a healthy respect for the ocean. I told you, didn't I, how he had to hang on to the overturned hull of the fishing boat for—well, I don't know for how long. Each time my father told us the story, it got longer and longer—four hours, six hours, a whole day. Sharks, too. My father said he worried about sharks—oh, I told you how my father said he knew Hemingway. My father said he used to run into Hemingway everywhere in Havana—at clubs, in casinos, in the hotel bars—and even the boat that overturned—my father said it was a much smaller world then—was the same boat Hemingway used to charter to fish for tuna and marlin. The name of the boat was the *Eleanora K*. I'll never forget this either because my father remembered, he said, that when he was in the water trying to hold on and keep from drowning the way the other two had—the captain and the man who baited the hooks and netted the fish—he, at the same time, was trying to think what the letter K could stand for. In a way, my father said, this was what saved his life, this was what kept him alive. Thinking of something, he said, was a way of not thinking about drowning, and my mother, when she heard my father say this, said: Oh, but darling, you are just accident prone. Some people are, you know, Molly. William was. So was Sam. Each time I asked Sam to hang up a picture or to fix something, he would drop a heavy tool on his foot or hit his thumb with a hammer. Or he would put his back out. Each time, too, Sam and I went on a trip, Molly, Sam's back would go out again, and Sam said he could not lift anything or carry my suitcase."

Molly said, "Claude-Marie put his back out. Claude-Marie says he can't play golf now."

I said, "Oh, but what I was saying was the K took my father's mind off his predicament. Like the time I was just telling you about when Sam and I were stuck in the Lincoln Tunnel and Sam said for me to try and relax and to think of something—

and you know what I did then, Molly? I started to recite things—poems. Poetry. I recited all the poems I knew by heart, the way I did later in the desert, the time we ran out of gas and the woman nursing her baby drove Jim back in the tow truck."

Molly said, "I told you how my mother used to lie on her chaise longue all day reading poetry and smoking these thin little cigarettes—come to think of it, they were Russian cigarettes. Who knows where she bought them in Charlottesville. I told you—Anastasia lived in Charlottesville, and I told you how my mother kept the book by Axel Munthe by the side of—oh, *The Story of San Michele* that's what the book is called. I just thought of it. Lily? Are you there, Lily?"

I said, "Oh, and poor Patricia in the overturned carriage in Anacapri."

Molly said, "Yes, this reminds me—the coat. Inez's down coat with the leopard spot pattern."

I said, "And Nora's new coat—have you seen it? A sheared beaver. Nora said she bought it on sale. You should feel it— soft as velvet."

Molly said, "Expensive."

I said, "You can't take it with you, was what I said to her, to Nora, I mean—oh, I know what you are thinking, Molly. You are thinking about Inez now—you are thinking about the money. Inez asked me—I didn't tell you this, Molly—Inez said she would also ask Nora, and I said to Inez: But, Inez, just think of their small crowded apartment and Ivan has not sold a painting in months. What about your own mother? Your mother's new husband, your stepfather, is a wealthy CEO, I said to Inez. This was a Sunday—I remember this distinctly, Molly—I had just walked in the door from the country, from upstate New York, and the phone was ringing.

Did I tell you how Leonard shares a house in the country with his partner, Howard? Howard Something-or-other. They each get to use the house on alternate weekends and Howard's girlfriend—I've never met her, Molly, and I've only met Howard once—is just like Sara, Price Junior's girlfriend, she is allergic to down and to all kinds of feathers. All the pillows in this weekend house, Molly, are made out of kapok, and kapok is not as comfortable. Oh, and did I tell you about Howard? About Howard's new company, the company Howard has started? A spit company. Yes, you heard me correctly. S-P-I-T is what I said. A company that collects spit for testing—now you have heard everything. But what was I saying? Oh, Inez, and the telephone was ringing, and you know me, Molly—I can never say no to people, I cannot say no to anyone, and I told Inez: No. No, I'm sorry, I said. I'm awfully sorry, Inez, I would if I could, but I cannot lend you the thousand dollars, was what I told Inez. I told her about my alimony, I told Inez about my rent. I can't remember what else I said. I said that they were going to raise the rent—oh, and guess what, Molly? They did. Isn't this funny? Isn't this ironic? They will raise the rent on this outrageous hole-in-the-wall of an apartment starting next month. Starting in June. Can you believe this? I got a letter in the mail last week saying that they were raising the rent ten percent. The letter said this could not be helped. Now, is this prescient or what? I ask you. I hadn't even thought of the rent, I just said the first thing that came into my head. Also, I had an instinct. No, not about the rent. About Inez. About lending Inez the money. I've had those instincts before, Molly—strong instincts—for instance, long before we stepped on board the plane to Marrakesh I knew that something was going to happen. I was right. When we got back, Sam and Felicia barely waited three weeks to get married. I should have known, Molly. I should have guessed. All men are liars, and Sam, don't forget, lied to me in Marrakesh, Sam lied to me in Fez—Fez was where it started, Molly. Fez, I'll never forget."

Molly said, "Yes, poor Inez."

I said, "No. Fez, Molly. Hello? I said, Fez."

Molly said, "Oh. Oh, Fez."

I said, "And Felicia is the perfect example—and I am not talking about Felicia's figure, if you like the athletic type, and if you like the type of woman who has made a career for herself risking her life taking photographs in places like the Middle East and Nicaragua—no, I am not talking about this."

Molly said, "Like Roberta, and I've always said, other people's sex lives are a complete mystery to me."

I said, "You're so right, Molly—I told you, Leonard. You would never know with Leonard. At first, I didn't know either. Hello?"

Molly said, "Yes, you didn't know, you said. It must be nearly near five o' clock in the morning, Lily."

I said, "Yes, and Leonard is quiet. I told Leonard: Never mind, honestly, I prefer staying home and reading a book. Oh, why am I trying to remember this now? Molly, why did I tell Leonard about the woman who gave me the pottery lessons—was it something to do with being celibate and living in a monastery? The truth is, I told Leonard, in my opinion, the ideal companion is a dog—a dog like Jason, I said,—a golden Labrador retriever. A dog, Molly, who obeys when you call him, a dog who knows how to lie quietly at your feet if you are reading, say—and Jason was like this, Molly. Jason knew almost before I knew myself what it was I was going to do and I told Leonard this. I did, Molly. I told Leonard all about Jason at Michelle's party. I told Leonard how Jason

would follow me around the house without getting under-
foot or in my way the way some dogs do so that you are
always almost tripping over them. But no, not Jason. Jason
had a sixth sense. Jason knew. In the mornings, too, Jason
knew when Sam and I were awake. Neither one of us had to
move or speak, Jason would stand up, wag his tail, stretch.
The way we breathed maybe. The other thing Jason loved
was to ride with us in the car. I took Jason with me everywhere and even if I had to leave him alone sometimes, while
I went shopping or while I went to visit someone—Sam's
mother, for instance. I told you, didn't I, Molly, how Sam's
mother lived in Cincinnati? Sam's mother wouldn't let poor
old Jason set foot in her house. I don't know how many
times I told Sam's mother how Jason was perfectly trained
and still she didn't believe me, and each time she had to
tell me the same old story again about how the last time
a dog had set foot in her house, the dog ruined her Aubusson
carpet. But the whole point of this, and what I told Leonard,
was how I had to leave poor Jason alone in the car and how
this was one of the worst things I have ever done in my whole
life and how this was negligent and how I will never forget
this."

Molly said, "I know, I know. Like the cat. Like Alicia
Thomas's cat, Lily. I'll never forget the cat, Lily."

I said, "No, no, Molly, this was not the same thing. I forgot.
I completely forgot. I left Jason locked up inside the car for
two and a half hours. I left Jason locked up inside the car
while I went to a movie. I had not intended to do this. I had
intended to be right back in just a few minutes, only I ran
into Marcelline—you've heard me speak of Marcelline,
Molly. Marcelline was the one who by the time she found the
lump in her breast her whole body was riddled with cancer.

But this was before this, and Marcelline said to me: Who cares what movie is playing, Lily, the theater is air-conditioned. I left the car parked in the sun—in the boiling sun. Ninety degrees in the shade that day. You don't know. You have never been to Cincinnati in the summer, have you, Molly? In August? The windows were shut—I told you, Molly—I was intending to come right back. Later, the vet said Jason must have panicked. You should have seen the inside of the car, Molly. The seats, the dashboard, the upholstery were all chewed up. A Volkswagen, Molly. A little yellow beetle— and you know how each time you slammed the door shut on this kind of car you created a vacuum and your ears popped. This was the trouble. The Volkswagen was made to be airtight. And speaking of never driving again. I remember, I told Sam, I liked how the Volkswagen was so maneuverable. I didn't care that the engine was in the back and that Sam said it was more dangerous this way. I told Sam I preferred driving the Volkswagen any day to driving his Mustang. Molly, I tell you, each time I drove Sam's Mustang, I felt as if the Mustang was getting away from me. My foot would barely touch the accelerator and, before I knew it, I would look down and I was doing over eighty. And, Molly, you don't know the Ohio State troopers—the Ohio State troopers are just as fierce as the French police if they catch you speeding. No — keep your Mustang, I told Sam, give me back my little yellow beetle. But what was I saying? Oh, yes, Jason. I was saying I told Leonard all about how when Marcelline and I came out of the movie—I told you already, didn't I, that it was a matinée? *Blow Up*—did you see *Blow Up*, Molly?—was the movie Marcelline and I went to. *Blow Up*, remember, was sort of a cult film in the sixties and it is about this photographer in London who discovers that he has inadvertently photographed a murder and he keeps enlarging and enlarging the photograph. Actually, I had seen *Blow Up* before, only Marcelline convinced me on account of the air-conditioning. The heat, I already said, and Marcelline had not seen *Blow Up* yet—and as I came out of the theater, I suddenly remembered. Oh, my God, I said. Oh, my God, Marcelline, the dog, Jason, and Marcelline said: Who? What are you talking about, Lily? Of course, Marcelline had no idea. Marcelline didn't know what I was talking about, and I started to run up the street towards my car—the little yellow Volkswagen. I knew, too, Molly. I knew long before I saw that the windows were all fogged over with Jason's breath that something had happened, that something was wrong, and there was Marcelline running right behind me shouting how I should slow down and how she was out of breath and how it was too hot to run like this, anyway. Funny, if only Marcelline had known then about the lump in her breast, things might have been different. Oh, and poor Jason. I was right, it was too late. You should have seen Jason's tongue, Molly. This was the worst part. Worse than seeing the seat and the upholstery. I'll never forget how Jason's tongue, Molly, was full of little holes with blood still in them that he had chewed there himself. You know what I did, Molly? I told Leonard this. I told Leonard this was what I did instinctively and without thinking and just like what's-her-name Marietta Tree when Adlai Stevenson had his heart attack in the street with her—remember that photograph, Molly? I got down on my hands and knees and I put my mouth right over Jason's—over his muzzle, Molly. I tried to give Jason mouth-to-mouth resuscitation just as if Jason was a person. The whole time, too, I could hear Marcelline behind me saying how if I didn't stop what I was doing I was going to catch hoof-and-mouth disease and die, and asking me when was the last time I had had my tetanus shot. While if you stopped to think about it, Molly, there was Marcelline herself with the cancer already spreading all over inside her, which again just goes to show you, doesn't it?"

Molly said, "The cat was different. Alicia Thomas's cat had a broken back, Lily. I had to put him out of his misery."

I said, "The strange thing—this was what I told Sam later —Jason was still breathing. Jason was still gasping for air when I got to the car. But Sam said he swore to me it was only a spasm. A reflex reaction—you know, like a chicken running with its head cut off or a dead shark closing his jaw on your leg. And this was what I also said to Leonard."

Molly said, "What? A shark, Lily? Lily, I thought you were talking about a dog, your dog—I must have missed something—missed something you said. Are you still talking about Inez?"

I said, "Yes. This is what my father said—even if the shark is dead, be careful—oh, and Inez. Inez, Molly, loved all animals. Inez loved dogs."

Molly said, "Inez loved cats."

I said, "Oh, and Inez loved her gardenia plants and I keep thinking, Molly, of how if only I had more light in this apart-ment, then I would call Price. Gardenias need a lot of light —I had a ficus tree once. Jim gave me the ficus tree for our anniversary—and you won't believe this—in less than a month the ficus tree's leaves had all turned yellow, the next month, the leaves were lying all over the carpet and you should have seen the mess. Jim accused me of not watering the ficus tree—oh, I know, I should have played music and like who said? Oh, Inez's mother said, I should have played Beethoven to it."

Molly said, "Please, don't play 'Für Elise.' Mozart, she said, which reminds me, in the morning I am going to call Claude-Marie about Inez's blue-and-white kimono. I am also going to ask Claude-Marie to ask Price what Fiddle stands for, so this will stop driving me crazy—oh, and what else? The airline ticket."

I said, "Jim said the ficus tree was symbolic. I told Jim how he was reading too much into it and how maybe the ficus tree was old, or how maybe the ficus tree was diseased when Jim bought it, or how maybe I didn't have a green thumb after all, or how, better still, maybe Jim should have asked me what I wanted for an anniversary present—a new—oh, Molly, I just thought of the story of Churchill and the radio. It's the story of how during the war Churchill was staying with some friends for the weekend, isn't it? And didn't Churchill receive a package with a radio in it? Now, I remember, since Churchill already owned a radio—Churchill probably owned several radios by then—Churchill gave the radio as a present to the son of his friends, the friends he was staying with then—a little boy. When the little boy turned on the radio, the radio blew up the little boy. This is the story, isn't it, Molly?"

Molly said, "Terrible—the same thing could have happened to the woman with the hand grenade if she had pulled the pin."

I said, "Yes, awful, and you'd think, wouldn't you, that Churchill or that one of his aides, after opening the package, would have also checked the radio—checked over the radio with a fine-tooth comb."

Molly said, "Yes—like me. You should see me, Lily, I am going through everything in this desk."

I said, "On the other hand, what if, say, Churchill himself had turned on the radio? What if Churchill had got blown up in 1941? Would England have continued to fight on in the war? Or would Hitler be ruling most of the world now? Or what if one of Churchill's aides or whoever was there looking after Churchill opened the package and he was the one who got blown up? This man, too, Molly, could have had a family—a handicapped mother, a dependent wife, several small children."

Molly said, "A child makes it worse. Think if it had been Bibi, Lily."

I said, "Yes, no—children, animals, tragic—Molly, I am just looking at my watch. It is after five o'clock in the morning. Soon it will be time to get up."

Molly said, "I *am* up, and the cat—no, no, I am not speaking of Alicia Thomas's cat, Lily. I am speaking of our cat here, Lily. I can't leave the cat in Connecticut, Lily. I was going to ask Inez."

I said, "That's the thing—who is going to look after the gardenia plants? No, no, not Price. No, not Fiddle, and not one of those kids—Price Junior and Matthew. Oh, if only I had more light here."

Molly said, "Yes, yes, soon it will be daylight, and if today is May twenty-fourth, then tomorrow is Thursday, which is the day I have to go to the dentist, Lily."

I said, "The way to figure this out, Molly, is to work backwards. If Leslie's wedding is on Friday, and Friday is May twenty-sixth, and today is Wednesday, May twenty-fourth, then you're right, your dentist appointment is on Thursday. Still, I can't believe what you said about Inez yesterday, which was May twenty-third, or how time goes by so quickly, and how long, for instance, since Jason died? Marcelline, of course, was still alive—Marcelline was standing right behind me as I was trying to give poor Jason mouth-to-mouth, and Marcelline was telling me about hoof-and-mouth disease—

but Marcelline died a year later, and I was still married to Sam then. Sam and I, I remember, went to Marcelline's funeral together, and I also remember how I told Sam he had to wear a suit and a dark tie."

Molly said, "Yes, of course."

I said, "Molly? Molly, are you paying attention to me? I remember Sam had just started to wear bow ties. Sam said how bow ties suited him better, and Sam had also smashed his thumb with a hammer, which was why he made me tie his bow tie for him. You should have seen me, Molly—we were nearly late to Marcelline's funeral."

Molly said, "I know, I know. Can you believe this, Lily? I am still looking for the interview."

I said, "I know what you mean. Once I start to look for something, I look and look until I find it. My ring—I told you how I looked all night. I looked everywhere, but at least I got the money back. I told you how I told the insurance company the ring was stolen—stolen from a hotel. I told them it could have been the maid. I said she could have been a Mexican. I know what you are thinking, only think of the insurance premium. But you know what happened next? Well —this was less than a year later—this was in the motel in Reno the night after we ran out of gas in the desert and I recited all the poems I knew by heart including *Friends, Romans, countrymen*—while I was waiting for Jim to come back in the tow truck with the woman who was breast-feeding her child—but what was I saying? Oh, the maid in the motel stole a dress from me. I have no idea what her nationality was, but who else had access to our room, and who else would want a dress? My blue dress was hanging up in the bathroom while we were having supper. You know, one of those drip-dry dresses—no, not the blue dress with the gold flecks in it from

Italy—a different dress, a French blue is, I guess, what you would call the blue of the dress, a blue Jim liked and that Jim said matched my eyes exactly, and I wore the dress every day on our trip—oh, and a blue, I bet, Matisse would have liked, Molly. A Matisse blue—Molly, you have not fallen asleep, have you? And at night when I took the dress off, I just washed it in the bathroom and, lo and behold, the next morning, the dress was dry."

Molly said, "I had a dress like this once, Lily. The dress wasn't blue. It was a cream color. A summer dress. Cotton. Percale. The French count gave me the dress. The French count knew my size—size six—not like Claude-Marie. Poor Claude-Marie. I told you how Claude-Marie bought me the red sweater that was the wrong kind of red and how I finally had to give the red sweater away to Madame Florisson's daughter-in-law."

I said, "Who, Molly? Madame Florisson? The name sounds familiar. Is Madame Florisson Bibi's piano teacher?"

Molly said, "No, no, Mademoiselle Boudemange is Bibi's piano teacher, Lily. Madame Florisson is the one who owns the bakery on rue du Bac—rue du Bac is just a few blocks across Boulevard Raspail from the house on rue Madame— and the bakery is the one with those wonderful lemon tarts. I get hungry just thinking about those wonderful lemon tarts. Lily, I told you, didn't I? I haven't had supper yet."

I said, "Molly, it's breakfast time nearly—oh, and Molly, how I envy you, how I really envy you, and this was exactly what I told Leonard: Leonard, I said, you have no idea how I want to go back to Paris, how I want to go back up the Eiffel Tower, how I want to visit those museums."

Molly said, "I told Claude-Marie the same thing, Lily. I told Claude-Marie don't fly Air India."

I said, "Air India—ha, ha. Yuri and the lobsters—I know I will never forget this story, Molly."

Molly said, "Only you can't always believe what Nora says—Nora may have made up the lobster part—just like you can't believe what Nora said about her sister, Mercedes, in the low-cut black dress."

I said, "Poor Mercedes nearly died of appendicitis—but what was I saying, Molly? I was saying how in Paris I want to look at art, how I want to visit museums—what is the name of the new museum that used to be a railroad station? The Musée D'Orsay, and who was I talking to recently? Oh, Malcolm. Malcolm was telling me about *his* idea for a museum, the scent museum, and what I told Leslie after she came back from Nicaragua was: I don't care what Malcolm talks about, I have always admired Malcolm's sculpture. Malcolm's sculpture is truly original, was what I said to Leslie, not like some of the sculpture you see nowadays, and like the exhibit I saw with Leonard—jars filled with paint. Paint from The White House, paint from all kinds of government buildings, and all the paint was off-white except for the paint from the Smithsonian building. The Smithsonian paint was a light pink color, and I said to Leonard: Is this a symbolic statement or what? But what was I saying? Oh, Malcolm. Malcolm's Masai. The Masai standing right behind the old couch Inez was always talking about and saying how she wanted to throw it out—the couch—and how instead, she wanted to buy a brand-new leather couch, and I kept telling Inez, no, not to. The couch, I told Inez, was an antique, unique, and, if she wanted my opinion, I said, I would throw out the rug. Do you remember the rug, Molly? I told Inez: Frankly, Inez, your rug is so faded, I can no longer tell if ever there was a pattern in it, and no wonder. No wonder, I said, with two kids roller-skating and skate-boarding all over the place. Two hyperactive kids, and poor Inez, she had her hands full with them. Inez could hardly ever leave the house without one of them breaking something or without one of them getting hurt or into some kind of trouble, and the people downstairs—no, not the playwright from Sri Lanka, another tenant—always complaining and telling Inez to tell those two kids to be quiet please, and to turn down the stereo—Price Junior and Matthew, and which one was the one who was nearly born in the car, Molly? I always got those two boys mixed up. To me, those two boys looked exactly alike. What do you call it when children are born so close together—Irish twins? My father and his brother were born exactly thirteen months apart, but I never met Uncle Denis—or if I did, I don't remember him. Uncle Denis, Molly, died of leukemia when I was only three years old."

Molly said, "Leukemia—and considering that no one writes letters any more, I have certainly managed to collect a lot of them—letters from Amy, letters from Suzanne in New Mexico, letters from Bibi, letters from Miss Mary—the artistic Miss Mary, not the Miss Mary who planted the vegetable garden—and a whole bunch of letters from my mother, to say nothing of all those old newspaper clippings Inez used to send me."

I said, "The rug I was telling you about, Molly—I told Inez if only Sam had not been pickpocketed, the rug from Marrakesh would have fit perfectly in my apartment—oh, but what did you say? I never write letters any more, either—it's easier to make a phone call. If I go away somewhere, I write a postcard. The funny thing is, half the time I am back from wherever I've been before the postcard arrives."

Molly said, "I told you, didn't I, Lily? I got a postcard from Alicia Thomas—a picture postcard of kittens."

I said, "Leslie said she sent everyone a postcard from Managua, and I told Leslie I haven't received her postcard yet, and I told Leslie wouldn't it be a coincidence if her postcard arrived on her wedding day, on May twenty-sixth. No one, I told Leslie, has received her postcards yet. Not Malcolm, not Ivan and Nora, Inez didn't either, as far as I know—I'm speaking of the day we played mah-jong with her friend the playwright from downstairs and from Sri Lanka and the day Kevin was standing in the doorway stark naked shouting at us, and Inez said then she still had not heard a word from Leslie. Leslie said she sent one to Fiddle and Price and she said she sent one to Yuri all the way over in Paris, and one to you and Claude-Marie, Molly, and oh—one to Roberta, too. And you know what, Molly? Roberta said she had received Leslie's postcard. Roberta said she received the postcard weeks ago—a postcard of a beach and of coconut trees. Do you believe her?"

Molly said, "Roberta? You must be joking, Lily."

I said, "I told Leslie: Leslie, I am certain I haven't received your postcard. Some things I remember, some things I just cannot forget. The only mail I've gotten recently is bills and oh, yes—I told you, Molly, that I received a letter saying how they were going to raise the rent ten percent and how they couldn't help it."

Molly said, "What did you say, Lily? Hello—I can hardly hear you. Some things I will never forget, either. I will never forget the cat, Lily, and I will never forget the plane crash. I have never seen so much smoke in my life. Claude-Marie actually had to turn the car around and drive back to Paris with his lights on."

I said, "You're right, Molly, some things are etched in my mind forever—Jason in the car with his tongue all chewed up, and the Moroccan man who threw the rock through our windshield."

Molly said, "Oh! Oh, Lily! Guess what! I found it! I found the interview with Matisse! Here it is! Right here! Oh, I knew I would! Thank God! Now I can go to bed. Now I can go to sleep."

I said, "Molly? Are you there—hello?"

Molly said, "Yes, yes—wait. I am looking at the interview again. Oh, God. Are you listening?"

I said, "Yes, yes, of course, I'm listening, Molly."

Molly said, "Yes. First, I am rereading it to myself. I haven't read this in such a long time. Oh, my God, I can't believe this, this was over thirty years ago. Now, I know. Matisse died in 1954."

I said, "In 1954? My mother—bless her heart—died in 1959, Molly. I was a freshman in college then. My father had to telephone me in the dormitory."

Molly said, "Matisse, Lily?"

I said, "It was a pay phone—I'll never forget—a pay phone upstairs in the hall of the dormitory, and another girl—a senior, I guess—was waiting for her boyfriend to call her, and she told me to make my phone call quick. Brief, she said. I'll never forget this. The way she said this to me: Make it brief."

Molly said, "But about Matisse, Lily."

I said, "Funny what you remember, isn't it? After I hung up the phone, I said to this girl, to the senior: Well, they just found my mother's body off the coast of Martha's Vineyard—was this brief enough for you?"

Molly said, "Oh, God, my God."

I said, "What, Molly? Molly, what's wrong?"

Molly said, "Nothing—it's just that the interview with Matisse is different from how I remember it, Lily."

I said, "Molly—different how? Hello?"

Molly said, "I don't know—it's hard to say exactly. I guess

I was just learning—learning how to speak French then. I mean—and you know how all this time I thought Matisse was talking about his art—well, he wasn't. He was just talking about—I don't know, listen to this—wait. No."

I said, "Molly, go ahead—read it, anyway. It doesn't matter. Go ahead and read it."

Molly said, "No. There is no point. Really, Lily. I swear it to you. Matisse was not saying anything profound, I assure you. I guess I forgot—he was pretty old by then. But how old was he, Lily? Well, I think, he was still painting a little, but he was confined to his wheel chair probably. Lily, this is too anecdotal—just listen to this, for instance—Matisse is telling the French-Canadian journalist exactly what he eats every morning for breakfast. Matisse says he has coffee with milk in it—hot milk, Lily—twice as much milk as coffee are the proportions Matisse gives. Matisse also says that he has a soft-boiled egg. Can you believe this? I swear this is true. I am translating the interview verbatim. According to Matisse, the soft-boiled egg has to be cooked three and a half minutes exactly if the egg is fresh. If the egg isn't fresh, it has to be cooked four minutes, is what Matisse says. Oh, I can't believe I forgot about this. Very frankly, Lily, I think I am tempted to throw all this junk away—the letters, the postcards, the newspaper clippings, all of it, the interview with Matisse included."

I said, "Oh, Molly, don't be too hasty. You never can tell. Maybe a biographer, someone writing a book about Matisse, might find the part about the three-minute boiled egg very significant. But what about the picture? Your picture? The photograph you took of Matisse with your Brownie camera?"

Molly said, "Oh—faded, it's faded. It's faded almost completely, Lily. Beyond recognition. I am not sure you could tell who it was unless you knew it was Matisse. You can just barely make out the white beard."

I said, "It's not on acid-free paper, that's why."

Molly said, "Matisse had very distinctive features, Lily. Matisse had a big nose. An aristocratic nose like what's-his-name's nose, the actor, and like the French count. The French count had a big nose, Lily."

I said, "You should see Leonard's nose, Molly. Leonard has a big nose. You've never met Leonard, have you, Molly? But what else does the interview with Matisse say? Besides about the boiled egg."

Molly said, "Something about what he thinks about us Americans—wait, let me read this again. Matisse is quoting something Picasso said—second-hand, Lily—actually what Gertrude Stein said Picasso once said: *Ils sont pas des femmes. Ils sont pas des hommes. Ils sont des Américains.* I remember this now, Lily, Matisse thought this was very funny, a real scream. Matisse laughed out loud. Oh, forget it. Then, I was probably more preoccupied with sleeping with the French-Canadian journalist and with worrying about whether my hair was curly enough. For God's sake, Lily, let's not forget, I was only eighteen at the time. I mean, I didn't understand all that much French or everything Matisse said to us."

I said, "Anyway, nothing is exactly the way you remember it, Molly. Did I tell you how I went back to visit the house I grew up in and how I was so disappointed? God, in a way, I wish I had never gone back. No. You should have seen the street, Molly. All the trees were gone. Chopped down, I guess. Lovely old oak trees. A real shame. The neighborhood, too, had changed completely. Gone completely downhill. The building Estelle Davidson had lived in, the building with the awning, for instance, that too, was gone, torn down probably."

Molly said, "Yes, yes—and who was it who said: You can't recreate the past, you can only invent it?"

I said, "Did Matisse say this in the interview, Molly? Did he? Because if Matisse said this in the interview, then I think the interview is worth keeping, Molly. Don't throw away the interview, Molly."

Molly said, "Yes, Lily."

I said, "And who knows, too, maybe one day Bibi will read the interview and Bibi will be able to tell everyone about how her mother met Matisse and about what Matisse ate for breakfast."

Molly said, "Do you think so, Lily? My God, speaking of breakfast! Oh, I think it's stopping raining, Lily. Can you believe this?"

I said, "No, it's still raining in New York. It's still drizzling. But let's hope it will stop raining for Leslie's wedding. Molly, did I tell you how they wrote their own service? How Victor is Jewish and Leslie is Catholic? Except who was it? Roberta? Was it Roberta who said that she heard it would rain through the weekend? But you're right, Molly, we should really get off the phone now. It's almost morning and this call is costing you a fortune. Still, thank God, you called, Molly. Thank God, we talked. Talking helps. Poor Inez. I still can't believe what you said. Inez was such a good friend. Inez was like you, Molly—Inez was one of my closest friends in all the world. Oh, poor Inez. And how did you say they found Inez? Standing up? Was this what you said, Molly? God, Inez. You said they found Inez propped up? Propped up like a what? What was it you said, Molly? A mop?"

Molly said, "A broom."

A NOTE ON THE TYPE

THE TEXT OF THIS BOOK WAS SET IN ELEC-
TRA, DESIGNED BY W. A. DWIGGINS (1880–
1956). THIS FACE CANNOT BE CLASSIFIED AS
EITHER MODERN OR OLD STYLE. IT IS NOT
BASED ON ANY HISTORICAL MODEL; NOR
DOES IT ECHO ANY PARTICULAR PERIOD OR
STYLE. IT AVOIDS THE EXTREME CONTRASTS
BETWEEN THICK AND THIN ELEMENTS THAT
MARK MOST MODERN FACES AND ATTEMPTS
TO GIVE A FEELING OF FLUIDITY, POWER,
AND SPEED.

COMPOSED BY CRANE TYPESETTING
SERVICE, INC.,
WEST BARNSTABLE,
MASSACHUSETTS
PRINTED AND BOUND BY FAIRFIELD
GRAPHICS,
FAIRFIELD, PENNSYLVANIA

DESIGNED BY GEORGE J. MCKEON